Pity

Poetry

PHYSICAL
PLAYTIME
PANDEMONIUM

As editor
100 QUEER POEMS

Pity

Andrew McMillan

CANONGATE

First published in Great Britain in 2024
by Canongate Books Ltd, 14 High Street, Edinburgh EH1 1TE

canongate.co.uk

3

For permission credits, please see p. 175

British Library Cataloguing-in-Publication Data
A catalogue record for this book is available on
request from the British Library

ISBN 978 1 83885 895 7

Typeset in Bembo by Palimpsest Book Production Ltd,
Falkirk, Stirlingshire

Printed and bound by CPI Group (UK) Ltd, Croydon CR0 4YY

MIX
Paper | Supporting
responsible forestry
FSC
www.fsc.org
FSC® C171272

for Margaret Goldthorpe
1928–2023

fallen in a heap
again
why do i keep
falling in a heap?

Alan Jackson

This is where we belong,
Who have inherited
The parish of the dead —

Peter Scupham

— shall I never get it clear, down in the soily waters.

Denise Riley

The net curtain moved like a skirt as Alex ducked his head underneath to check the dark street. The magazine was thrown down on the settee, open at the middle; a slowly collapsing tent. The road and the room were quiet.

Alex's hand was shaking slightly as he went back to the copy of *Rustler*. Pulling it towards himself with one of the inside pages, it fell open on a woman. His first thought was that her hair reminded him of his mother's.

Flicking through the pages to try and rid his mind of that image, there were more women; sometimes in a bra, sometimes not, sometimes straw-blond with black roots, sometimes with their legs spread. Some seeming to look directly at Alex, or the curtains and houses behind him. One page had a couple who seemed to Alex to be colliding together, like two kids jostling in a playground. It was like a comic book, he thought; sequential panels where the woman lost her clothes, and then the man, and in the final window, in the bottom right-hand corner of the page, Alex saw, for the first time, the female body.

He leaned forward, as though the image might fade. He remembered that the lad who'd passed him the magazine in school had said this was the bit that *really got him going*. Alex had nodded along, not really sure what the boy meant, but knowing it must connect somehow to the strange heaviness he felt in his stomach as the man's trousers puddled around his ankles, and the woman leaned back over a desk. In the corner of the room the TV played; a man in a suit nodded at the camera, the theme music of the local bulletin started, and a sombre reporter beamed in from a club Alex half recognised as he glanced up. He heard the word *survivors, rescue* but stood up to turn it off, not wanting it to feel like there were other people there, watching.

Back at the settee, Alex undid his trousers and scooched them beneath his bum. He didn't know what to do next. He saw in one of the frames what the man was doing with his hand as he looked at the woman. He'd seen boys in his class make the same shape with their hands when they were shouting at each other during P.E. All Alex could think to do, in that moment, was hold himself.

He slipped his free hand beneath his boxer shorts and cupped himself in his palm, the way he sometimes did when he was falling asleep. He thought he could feel his heart beating down there.

The woman was hairier than he'd imagined she would be. So was the man, a thick rug of it across the chest and stomach. His ribs weren't visible from the side, but he wasn't fat either. It seemed to Alex that the man had an entirely adult body, and clearly one which drove women wild. That was the kind of body he'd get as he got older, he told himself.

Alex didn't hear his brother's footsteps until they were right beside his head; he felt a hard right hand to the side of his ear.

Alex jumped up immediately, pulling his hand from his underwear and sending the woman and the man and the rest of the pages of the magazine onto the carpet.

'What're you doing, you perv? Mum'll be home soon.' Brian's voice seemed to waver more than usual on that last remark; they weren't used to being home alone this late, and when she'd hurried out earlier, grabbing her coat almost as an afterthought, she had said they could get chips if they want, there was a bit of money in the drawer, not to open the door for anyone.

'You little perv,' Brian repeated.

Alex began to explain about Tommy, the boy in his class who'd shown him the magazine and then let him take it home, and that he was only looking at it to see what it was, to maybe take his mind off things, you know. Brian cut him off mid-sentence.

'She's well nice, isn't she?' he said as he picked up the magazine. It seemed, in the way Brian had asked the question, that it didn't need a response.

Brian joined him on the settee and sat closer than Alex had expected; the magazine picked up now, and sitting across both their laps. Brian continued to ask him questions or point out pictures, using words Alex had never heard his brother use before.

The extra years had given Brian a few inches in height, a deeper voice, and so Alex was forced to tilt his head upwards to check the expression on his brother's face as he flicked through the pages. It was one of deep concentration.

After a couple of minutes of waiting for his heart rate to return to normal, Alex put his hand back down into the warmth between his legs, and held himself. Brian did the same, shuffling to adjust on the settee.

They sat like that for what seemed to Alex an age. One of them and then the other turning a page, using a finger to silently point out something of interest. At some point, Alex wasn't sure when, Brian reached over and put his arm around his younger brother's shoulders, in the same way he did when he'd scored the winning goal during a weekend's kickabout on the top field.

He steps out into the long corridor of early dawn; the street stretching downwards, pointing him to where he's headed. It's Monday, and the weekend is still unshaven stubble in his mind. Above, the sky is a solid lump of cloud and three doors down Pat is just closing his front door. Another few doors on there will be Harry and then Frank, and as they all turn the corner together Skip will already be ahead of them and each of them will briefly consider running after him and then think better of it. Nobody speaks; they incline their heads as someone else joins them and then keep on walking. More and more men fall out of their houses, like dominoes, their faces not yet blackened. Someone whistles; someone else coughs. Occasionally some stop, and lean for a moment on the low wall of a garden, pretending they need to double-check their snap tin or enjoy a long drag on their roll-up, sputtering the smoke out into the cold air in shallow breaths. Nobody waits for them, they just keep on walking. The village, on their shoulder now, still asleep, not watching the migration of tired bodies. One of the men once said he thought he could hear the coal ticking. Another man told him to stop talking daft. And beneath their feet, a mile down, history; waiting to be hacked into chunks and pulled out.

surveillance: CCTV

The head of security liked to boast that there were two sets of eyes on every wall. Here, Ryan had all those eyes in front of him; the flickering bank of screens, their static like rain on a hundred small windows.

Simon's words from the night before still stung as he sat down; it was the way they'd seemed rehearsed, the way he'd flung them at him, just as Ryan was leaving that morning: 'either come to the show or don't come back'.

Technically Ryan was only meant to review the camera footage to help with filing incident reports, but he'd be quick, and nobody would ask. He could bring up more than one at once.

The tapes got auto-wiped after thirty-one days, unless there was a particular incident the police asked them to save and store pending further investigation. It meant that the first time he'd seen Simon was about to be deleted, consigned to history. They'd messaged a bit on Grindr, and it was Simon who'd said something about popping into the shopping centre to try and get a glimpse of him. And still, when Ryan had spotted him, he hadn't seemed real – suddenly three-dimensional after the flat screen of the phone, like a story come to life.

Camera 4 sat just above the large TK Maxx, angled so it faced out into the gangway of shops, and Ryan knew the timestamp that would take him straight to the footage where he was able to first glimpse Simon, walking briskly, plastic Boots bag swinging in his hand, yellow lanyard bouncing on his chest.

Ryan zoomed in on the contents of the bag, bringing things into relief – the weight of a can of something fizzy at the bottom, the contours of a plastic-wrapped sandwich.

Ryan knew the footage off by heart. Camera 5, angled just above the toilets, tracked him as he moved through the centre. Simon glancing sideways, then stopping, leaning back against the wall of half tile, half cracked plaster. He was almost out of the frame, but leaned down to look into his phone so the top of his shaved head came back into shot. He looked up again. Then back down.

When Ryan brought the footage of Camera 7 up onto the screen, the one that sat just above the vape shop, he got his own back, black suit jacket stretched across the shoulders, and he watched himself looking out beyond the benches, and the empty expanse that followed them. Every so often he turned his head right or left, but mainly he was just there, looking straight out and over.

On Camera 5, Simon looked up again, this time for slightly longer. The face blurred but the way the pixels arranged themselves suggesting a slight smile. Then the head back down again, the bag between his white trainers, the white handles drooped over like an unwatered house plant. Two fingers typing. Looking down at his phone, and then lifting it up, quickly, pressing his thumb into the screen, and lowering it again. Another pixelated smile and then Simon picked up the bag and walked off and out of the view of Camera 5.

Camera 12 showed him walking through the side exit into the high street. Bag bouncing against his thigh. Lanyard swaying against his chest.

Ryan stopped playing the footage. Reached momentarily for his phone, but stopped and found himself looking at the familiar theatre of his face, reflected in the blank screen in front of him.

To get ready he had to lose himself, and then find himself as someone else. That's how he'd described it to Ryan on their first date, who'd sort of nodded along though Simon sensed he didn't really get it. He supposed that was fair enough. To Ryan, hiding was about getting away with something, covering your face up with a scarf as you grabbed what you could fit in your pockets and ran out of a shop, hoping you might be able to sell some of it later. Ryan understood disguise, trying to hide, but it was different to lose yourself in something that was hyper-visible; the way you could lay something over the surface, and in the gentle touch that took, come to know better what was underneath.

The flat had been new when Simon had moved in; built on the car park of the old petrol station in front of the football ground. It's where they'd left the car for the home matches his dad had taken him to when he was younger, and now what had been the forecourt was a thin strip of town houses and Simon would stand at the Juliet balcony on alternate Saturdays and curse at the matchday fans using his parking space, even though he didn't have a car.

In the bedroom Simon was spreading out the things he'd managed to find for Saturday's gig; the new lace-front, the two-piece suit and the plastic pearls.

He kept glancing at his phone, but it didn't light up.

He knew the easiest thing to do would be to just put on a glittery frock and his big wig and sing a couple of the old favourites, 'River Deep', 'Proud Mary', and then maybe he could get everyone up doing 'Born To Hand Jive'. It would be good, harmless fun. A straight man's idea of what a gay drag act might do. For a first event for the club, and for Trip trying it out, it would probably be safest.

But Simon felt like he should have something to say, something he couldn't say when he had to think about earning money, keeping his regular slot on the evenings he worked over in Sheffield. He didn't just want to do what his dad or Brian or Trip probably expected, he wanted to surprise them.

He got out his sketchpad, where three looks were all planned out. He'd tell the story of the strike, and end singing 'Ding Dong! The Witch Is Dead', like he'd watched people do on the news when they announced that Thatcher had died. He'd put the songs he wanted onto a playlist and get Trip to start playing it at just the right time so that he could lip-synch his way through everything.

He'd started to make a set-list of songs. He hadn't got very far, despite only having a few more days, but there was one that he'd seen some people singing in some news clips of the strike, in the quieter moments, when they weren't burning effigies of *Maggie Maggie Maggie*. He'd only caught the first few lines:

> *We are women*
> *we are strong*
> *we are fighting*
> *for our lives*
> *side by side*
> *with our men*
> *who work the nation's*
> *mines*

and then this last hurrah that seemed to be drowned out in cheers and whoops whenever it was reached

> *and it's here we go here we go*
> *for the women of the working class*

He thought some of them must have sung it back then, even if he hadn't known the song until the other night. He could picture it now: miming along, people singing in the audience, and maybe some of them would be tearing up, and they'd be tapping their glasses on the tables, and they'd be thinking of themselves, when they'd sung that, or when their wives or sisters or mothers had sung that, and stood out in the freezing cold in rows, like a chorus line.

He began to sway around the bedroom. The tannoy at the ground was testing its evacuation message before the weekend's local derby.

They'd be clapping along, all of them, maybe some of them already in a good mood if Barnsley had won; Trip at the bar, his dad and Brian, and all the regulars.

and it's here we go here we go

he'd be miming

for the women of the working class

and he'd open his mouth and move his lips as though he was straining to hit that final note and then he'd bring down his hand that he'd clenched in a fist over his head, and maybe some of them would be standing, maybe they'd stomp their feet so that even the traffic outside was drowned out. And he'd bring his hand to his hip and he'd pull and the outfit and the Velcro would rip off and he'd be wearing black tights, with holes in them, and a leotard the green of AstroTurf, and he'd pull the rest over his head to reveal a vest that said *Maggie*, just once, in capital letters, and he'd put a pointed hat on, and he'd be Her, come back as a witch, and he'd nod across to Trip that it was time for the next track.

The voice inside the ground was calling for *Mister Sands*, was telling him to *report to the Safety Office*.

Simon danced silently around his room.

Fieldnotes: Glory

The two greatest achievements of the town's football team are as follows: in 1912, the year the *Titanic* sank, they won the FA Cup, and at the end of the 1996/97 season they were promoted to the Premiership, where they spent one season. One of our team members has revisited several recordings of matches from the latter season, some on *Match of the Day*, the weekly magazine roundup show, when, unless a 'top six' team was being played, the highlights of the town's game were invariably already shown in the programme's introductory sequence and the game discussed last, just before the end; others were revisited from live TV coverage.

One phrase which was noted as coming up a lot, in various different iterations, was 'they (another team) should be doing better against a team like this'. It was said by commentators, pundits, by managers after a game where a draw had been secured or a loss endured. We have discussed how this could be both a reflection on the perceived strength of the team's squad (financially and physically weaker than many others) but also on the town itself; the top four teams that year were two London-based clubs, Arsenal and Chelsea, and two based in some of the largest northern population hubs, Manchester and Liverpool. The league winners that season, Arsenal, come from a population centre over seventy-five times greater than that of the town. 'We should be doing better against a town like this.'

Another member of our team has been researching an incident that has not lodged itself into the national consciousness, and there is little or no mention of it in local history files either. In 1908, on a Saturday at the beginning of the year, sixteen children died and at least forty were seriously injured when, during a penny performance for children at the Public Hall now colloquially known as the Civic, the size of the crowd meant that some children began to be crushed against the first-floor railing.

In order to alleviate the press of bodies, the attendants encouraged the young audience to make their way downstairs to the main floor, but the panic and rush down the narrow staircase led to people falling, and being crushed under the weight of other panicked children. There is evidence that newspapers worldwide reported the story, with graphic details of the injuries and deaths. We wonder why it is with some places that whenever they appear in the national or international press, it is for tragic or violent reasons. What must this do to the perceptions of a place, and to residents' self-perception of the place they inhabit? A member of our team draws a not unwarranted comparison to the notion of a 'failing school', as termed by the local authority or Ofsted inspectors. It is often a self-fulfilling prophecy: a school must first identify itself as failing, or accept that terminology from outside onto itself, in order to qualify for more funding and more support to help its own students. These students are then stigmatised as having gone to an inferior school or as having come from a deprived area. Their achievements, like those of the local football team, are always 'over-achievements'; the tragedies and violence of the town are international news, its successes are not.

Like a roundabout at the centre of a disused road, the club had stayed constant while things around it shifted. The pub that was a church. The house that was flats. The corner shop that was a hairdresser's and then a nail bar and then an e-cig café. Almost every month, Brian thought to himself, there was another old layer of the street peeled back, something new waiting underneath.

He'd asked what the point of it was several times and he still didn't know. The flyer he'd picked up in the club a few weeks before had mentioned a 'week of recollection', with 'three fun and interactive sessions'; the fact there'd be refreshments and food was in bold and underlined. Still, now that he was here, he didn't know why he'd agreed to come along and listen, or why they'd come at all, what any of it had to do with Trip's club or the patient woman he'd seen a few times posing for photos outside the food bank that she helped to run in the centre of town.

He'd asked again, and still not quite understood the answer. They repeated that they were a group of researchers and academics from the university. That the fiftieth anniversary of the disaster had prompted them to stage a 'week-long discursive intervention to explore the history and inheritance of social trauma'. That there weren't any 'set outcomes, they just wanted to see what happened, and to record their own reflections and insights as they went along'.

Brian remembered the event, had seen it on TV, on the news at the time.

They'd asked him to tell them about where they were sitting now, about the club, but also about the town, what he'd done there, where he'd worked. It felt too close to something at the Job Centre, and so he'd mumbled a few bits about the pit, about the strike, and then he'd gone quiet again, scuffing his shoes on the floor.

A couple of the other men spoke up a bit more; he knew one of them as a regular, and the woman tried to encourage them, but in a way which felt like pulling the words out of them, against their will.

He'd seen a couple of them exchange glances, in black t-shirts and nice jeans, no jumpers or coats, despite the fact it was cold in the central space of the club, the heating not programmed to come on until eleven and none of them sure how to change it.

The younger one of them reached into a rucksack and brought out a stack of plain white index cards. He put them down onto the table as though some sort of magic trick. A set of pens followed.

He was told they wanted him to try and map out the place he was from, as he remembered it from when he was young. They didn't want the real names of the streets, or the shops, they wanted what he'd called them; they wanted him to create a personal map of the area. They said that was a good place to start, a good way of letting them get to know the town.

The cage is what he hates most, crowded together into a space no bigger than a front porch. The expanse of the weekend closing. Being so cramped and close up, descending and smelling the other men, their Sundays, and their lack of sleep and their wives and their children and last night's supper. He'd shower after his shift, and hadn't washed at home, and so the night still hangs heavy on him. Watching the earth pull up around him, through the bars, he feels like an animal, travelling beneath the wooden beams, the lights, and then coming to a stop and a man stepping forward, like a school teacher to a gate, to open up and let them through. Each time it takes his eyes a while to adjust to the new darkness, like waking up all over again. And then they walk. Headlamps pointing the way into the tunnels and there isn't much talking, something like a gathering of breath, readying for the black wall they eventually meet, which never seems to recede no matter the hours they put in with their tools. At least out of the lift he's free to move his limbs, to swing and to pick and to break. Sometimes he feels like a germ, dismantling something from the inside out. Sometimes the noise of the belts and the drills is so loud it's as if he can hear the gears of the earth turning and turning.

surveillance: CCTV

Ryan had done a quick walkabout on the upper concourses, but it was quiet; just the usual Monday afternoon bench-sitters and people slipping in and out on breaks from work. Now, back in the quiet chasm of the control room, he was alone. He could see on the live feed from a couple of the cameras that Ray and Steve were down on the lower floor, near the entrance, talking to someone who had their head down, and hood up. As supervisor he should probably radio in to see if things were OK, but he was too tired, too worn down from the fight with Simon the night before.

He should text him, Ryan knew, but he couldn't bring himself to finish typing. Every time he picked up his phone he lost the words. He knew Simon might be seeing him typing, the three tiny circles of light hovering momentarily in an empty speech bubble and then disappearing. What had they even fought about? He couldn't remember. Except, of course, he could.

He searched in the system and brought up the video from Camera 11, the one that faced the café that was really just a kiosk and some scattered chairs in the middle of a gangway. Their first date. Everything had happened so quickly, as though they were running out of time somehow. Simon messaging him again on Grindr after he'd spotted him working, arranging to come back to the Alhambra the next day for lunch, the two of them sitting there, around a small table that looked more like patio furniture, Ryan with his coat on despite the heat, so people didn't think he was working. So they wouldn't be interrupted.

And there they were, uninterrupted, on screen. The camera was on their right and so the lower half of their bodies and their legs were visible under the table, both turned at angles to avoid touching. Black suit trousers and polished shoes on one side, grey fitted jeans and white trainers on the other. Every so often, as Ryan watched, their knees would silently touch under the table, and bounce back. Their legs shifted position, a foot tapped, both their bodies adjusted themselves in a way which suggested they were having an animated conversation, though Ryan couldn't remember what about.

A third body came over to the table, a black apron tied around a midsection, and an arm reaching over with a bottle of coke, a mug of tea. Ryan knew they'd sat there for the entirety of his lunch break and so he sped the footage up a bit, at one point his hand on the grey jeans, then a figure moving past at the edge of the camera's eye, and a hasty retreat. Their legs close together again, knees touching and not moving away.

The third body arrived into shot again, moving slightly quicker now, on double speed. Another mug of tea, another coke, and then a jerk of an arm, liquid spilling, the grey jeans suddenly upright, a small puddle of milky tea growing on the floor. Ryan standing up now too, him and Simon shuffling out of the way while a mop came into view and then out and then in again, the tea slowly soaked up, wiped away.

Then the two of them returning to the table, Simon angling his chair more to the side now, so their legs were closer under the small table. In the control room Ryan watched as Simon brought out his phone, held it up, moved it over to him so he'd had to shuffle over a bit to see what he was being shown. Ryan's hand now on Simon's thigh, on his grey jeans, a hand moving in a small circle, as though over an invisible wound. Simon's white trainers hooked behind the black suit trousers of Ryan. The two pairs of legs staying close. The grey against the black, like a sky on the edge of a storm. The hand circling and circling until another hand slipped beneath the table, to hold it. Simon only looking at Ryan. Ryan turning around briefly to look directly at the camera. And here Ryan was, now, looking back at himself.

They seemed quite pleased with him, Brian thought, and he'd even gotten into it more towards the end, remembering the Rec, and Mr Mawi's Shop, and the Old Bridge. He'd put each name onto a square and then placed it where he imagined it would go if he were hovering above it, looking down. They really seemed to like that, he could see them writing things, exchanging glances with each other.

'So this here,' one of them said, pointing at one of his cards, 'this is one of the Darfield Playing Fields?'

He didn't know what they meant, he'd never heard it called that before, and so he just repeated that no, it was the Rec. They asked him not to put the names of the streets or the numbers of the houses, but to see if he could remember who lived there, and of course he could. His parents' house, the allotments that ran down the back of the terraced row opposite, Mrs Moody's, the houses of the aunties who weren't really aunties, Frank's house, Rob's house, the school. He couldn't understand why they'd find any of this interesting, they didn't know any of these people, and sometimes he didn't even remember second names, certainly didn't know anything they'd gone on to do after he'd forgotten about them, or they'd moved away. They existed only in the few years that he was trying to map, and there was something in that act he had started to enjoy, almost as though he was walking down those streets again, rather than shifting cards around the sticky wooden top of one of the club's longer tables.

They asked him about some of the things he hadn't filled in; his own street was a mouth with half its teeth missing, and he said he just didn't remember. 'Would you remember all of this about where you're from?' he asked them, and they didn't reply. He asked them why any of this was important. He thought they wanted to know about the strike, and about that specific day, about what it had felt like. He said he could tell them loads about striking if they wanted but they said maybe they'd get to it later. They said this seemed to be going well for now, that they should keep at it. He asked them again, why though, just as the woman was bringing in biscuits and plates of sandwiches wrapped in tinfoil. They said something about the import-ance of local memory in understanding a place. The regular, who'd sat quietly all the way through, only writing down a couple of street names and a couple of nicknames for local shops which they'd clearly rather he hadn't, spoke up then, saying 'You're not local, though, so how would you understand?' as he removed the covering from the sand-wiches like someone removing their cap for a passing hearse.

★

As Brian gathered with them at the buffet table he immediately felt awkward at their attempts to make small talk. They asked him which pit he'd worked in, whether it was the same one as his dad, what his son did. He answered in low grunts or not at all, 'Houghton Main', his brother had been there too, 'No son, but a nephew. It was a call centre for the gas,' he thought, '. . . or was it taking bets now, they kept shifting the teams around but it paid well, regular hours,' and then he went back to the sandwiches. They asked about the football, but he said he didn't really follow it. His nephew lived by the ground, though. They got distracted by the regular then, who was telling them about the plans the council had for the big park in town. Seven hundred houses, the regular was telling them, they'll all be stuck cheek by jowl, won't they, no gardens, no space. 'Just like terraces, I guess,' one of them said, and the regular had scoffed 'But without knowing any of the neighbours' names. They'll all be off to work in Leeds, or Sheffield, they'll hardly speak to each other.' They nodded in agreement, though he could tell they didn't really agree, or weren't really listening. 'What does your brother do now?' one of them had asked. 'He's divorced,' Brian had replied, without meaning for that to be his answer. 'It must have been hard, when everything happened, the emotional toll as much as the financial one . . .' 'It wasn't the strike,' Brian cut in, 'it's because he's . . .

well, it's just, some things don't work out, do they? Not everything is because of something, you know.'

He glanced back to the table. It was strange seeing his past flattened and laid out like that, as though someone had unfurled a tablecloth of it. He hadn't thought about some of those friends for years. They hadn't really left; he supposed he could keep in touch with them if he tried. He'd occasionally see them in town or on the bus and they'd nod to each other, or say hello, but that was about it. A few of them he'd worked with, or stood on the lines with in the eighties, but even them he never really chatted to.

One of them came over, holding a camera phone, and seemed about to take a picture when he noticed him. 'Don't let me disturb you, just wanted to get a picture of all your great work before it gets muddled up.' He glanced up at him and tried to smile. Their enthusiasm grated.

'I could always do it again for you,' Brian said, 'though it might be different next time.'

The one with the camera perked up at this. 'That's interesting, isn't it, the way that memory shifts so rapidly. How we can suddenly decide we were wrong.'

He shrugged. He didn't know. He took a sip from the polystyrene cup of lukewarm tea.

'I didn't say wrong,' he said.

Fieldnotes: The School

Whilst some of the team have been engaged at the club working with residents of the town, others of us have taken the time to visit a local school. We arrive at a turbulent time. The school has just been placed in special measures, and is under intense scrutiny from the local community over perceived anti-social behaviour which is spilling out into the village. One of the many criticisms from the local authority inspectors is of the language that teachers use in classrooms. They report that 'correct' English is not being modelled to the students. As a result the school has put up barriers, metaphorically and bureaucratically, to protect staff and students from outside scrutiny.

We meet with the headteacher, whom we have been keen to include in our project. Originally, we had proposed a series of collaborative workshops with Year 7 students, in which they would work with our project poet, and a musician, re-writing local history to centre their own experiences. The headteacher was initially happy for this to go ahead as long as our plans showed how the work would map onto the Year 9 academic expectations. Another idea we proposed was to turn control entirely over to the students. They would each develop a presentation based on something they were passionate about (a computer game, a sports team, a singer), and use our skills to help them craft the talk; we would be in service to them. This was designed to completely re-orientate the classroom, and to re-centre the knowledge within the space. The headteacher rejected this as he didn't think the students would respond well to the freedom, and the work proved impossible to fit within syllabus requirements. We left our meeting with the headteacher unsure of whether we would be able to work with them on the project. We found the school to be suspicious of academics, which is understandable. When Michael Gove said we've 'had enough of experts' his words were met with horror and derision within universities such as ours, but here, in places like this, where 'experts' are held responsible for low-wage, low-esteem and low-potential lives, the phrase rang true.

The school has had enough of experts. They've also, as it happens, had enough of artists; the last time an artistic intervention had been staged at the school, a group had received funding to work on site on the issues of authority and power. They proposed taking down all the non-load-bearing walls in the school to create, as much as possible, an 'open-plan dynamic learning environment'; there would be no distinct classrooms, no differentiation between year groups, no staff room. The artists said that their intervention was challenging notions of order and regulation, that learning should be fluid, and unconstrained. The teachers just wanted the students to get 5 GCSEs. Their parents just wanted them to get jobs.

Sometimes, when Alex is at home, sitting on his settee, this is what he remembers. The large black furnace of his old school sports hall, him and his mate Judd, page three of a newspaper crumpled like aged skin on the floor, their trousers and underpants around their ankles, one hand on themselves, one hand against the wooden slats to steady them. Both looking down, both determined not to be caught looking at the other.

Then the shoe to the back of the knee, and Alex scrambling on the floor to cover himself up, tangled in his own clothes and the dirt and the shredded page. A voice shouting fuckingdirtyfaggots, a voice shouting fuckingpervs, another shoe, this one to the back of his head, before the dust kicked up blurs his vision too much, Judd running off, jumping the fence, away into the park.

Then the headteacher's office, a serious low voice saying 'We know how hard it must have been, we know you miss him, we want to help.'

Sometimes, when Alex closes his eyes he can still see the stains on his trousers as he looks down, the sharp edges of the headteacher's desk. That serious low voice again. 'There are things best done at home. There are things best kept inside.'

He steps out into the long corridor of early dawn; last night's rain a damp carpet underfoot, the static of drizzle in the air. Above, the sky is a threadbare sock of grey, and three doors down Pat is just closing his front door. Another few doors on there will be Harry and then Frank, and as they all turn the corner together Skip will already be ahead of them and each of them will briefly consider running after him and then think better of it. Nobody speaks; they incline their heads as someone else joins them and then they keep on walking. More and more men fall out of their houses, the weekend like fluff in the bottom of their pocket that they can't quite reach. Someone whistles; someone else coughs. Occasionally some stop, and lean for a moment on the low wall of a garden, letting their bodies catch up with their minds. Nobody waits for them, they just keep on walking. The village, on their shoulder now, still asleep, not watching the migration of tired bodies. One of the men once said he thought he could hear the coal sighing. Another man told him to stop talking daft. And beneath their feet, a mile down, black diamond; waiting to be polished up, and sold.

Simon fumbled with the keys, trying to remember which one Trip said was the one for the shutter and which for the front door; he squinted at the alarm code written on the back of his hand, illuminated under the security light.

Even though Trip had said he could come in early on Tuesday, before they opened, and before Simon was due in at the call centre and long before his evening in Sheffield, it still felt illicit to be crouched down, his back lit up by the occasional passing car.

The shutter clattered up and made Simon wince; it sounded like a huge machine lurching into life. Once he was through the door, he punched *1912* into the beeping box. It was the last time Barnsley had won the FA Cup, Trip had told him, like that would help him remember. Then he stood in the doorway for a moment, trying to think where the lights were.

The space looked bigger in the half-light, the shadows of the barstools and the stage messing with the proportions of the walls. He found the white tablets of the light switches and flicked them on.

He left his jacket lying across one of the stools and stepped, in his vest and yoga leggings, to the back of the room. He counted the paces to himself as he walked around each of the tables, some of them still pushed together from some sort of event the day before, but most of them arranged, as they would be that weekend, cabaret-style. Simon tried to draw a map of the room in his head, imagining which tables he'd have to swish sideways to miss. Once he got to the stage, he took his phone out from his pocket and plugged in the jack lead from the CD speaker system.

Trip hadn't been sure that would work and offered to burn the songs onto a CD, but Simon had assured him that it would. That Saturday, when he began, he wanted it to be a surprise.

From the stage he could see himself in the mirror behind the bar; tiny, a small speck in the harsh lights of the club. The movements of his limbs didn't register back there, in the deep recesses of the room.

Make sure they sit close, Simon thought to himself. He pressed play on the first song, Beyoncé's 'Hello', and ran over to the door of the men's toilets, where he'd decided he'd emerge from. He started pacing out slowly, back towards the stage, imagining waving and speaking to the audience as he went. The main bit of the song kicked in before he arrived and so he started it again, and tried speeding up a bit, bursting out of the door with the stick figure of the man on it, and then striding with purpose. He managed to get up the steps just as the song kicked into a higher gear. He tried it again, and again; continuously emerging from the door and striding and arriving just before anything happened, and then stopping.

He'd found a good enough audio of a group of women singing 'Women of the Working Class' as part of some event up in Durham and, after last night spent swearing at his laptop, had managed to mix it with something that YouTube had called an 'industrial soundscape', which was mostly silence except for sudden rises of banging machinery, or clanking parts.

He'd decided he'd deliver the speeches himself. It started with Her 1987 Section 28 bit from the conference, the one he'd watched over and over again. That voice she had, it seemed so performed, caught between trying to drop an octave and trill upwards and be free.

This is how he saw it going. The soundscape would start, and at first there would be silence, the odd droning sound heard in the distance, no louder than a bus going by outside. He'd step forward, dressed in the iconic two-piece, over-sized wig and pearls, to make sure people really got it.

'Children are being taught that they have an inalienable right to be gay,' he would say. 'All of those children are being cheated of a sound start in life – yes, cheated.'

The soundscape in the background would begin to get louder, shouts of men, the sounds of heavy machinery like giant metal bodies colliding. He'd let the sounds hang in the silence. He'd walk to the back of the stage and pick up one of the placards he was making, the handles of them ripped from pallets he'd found. Daubed in red would be *The Lady's Not For Turning*, and he'd say those words to the audience, louder now, drowning out the sounds of industry behind him. Then he'd wink, although he wasn't sure if they'd see that under the wig, he'd need to practise in front of the mirror, and just as the industrial sounds and the shouts from the soundscape got louder, he'd turn around the sign and reveal the other side of it:

This Turn Is Not A Lady

He was proud of that one, and paused a moment in the walk-through to allow for the imagined laughter and cheering. Then the swell of voices would start to fade in over the soundscape. He'd prop the sign up, joke facing outwards, and begin to march on the spot, miming to the swell of voices that were now the only sound on the track.

He hoped people might join in. He hoped people might stand up.

As Simon walked back across to his phone, he remembered the time he'd left his mobile in the temporary classroom where they were taught history in secondary school; someone had picked it up and read out the text messages he'd been sending to another boy. He'd refused to go to the next lesson. He'd had to tell a teacher he was gay. The teacher paused momentarily, looked up to the Styrofoam ceiling tiles, and then whispered 'fuck Thatcher' before turning back to reassure him as he sobbed. Simon still remembered that, it came back to him every so often, when the wheel of memory dredged it up and brought it into the light and then sunk it down inside of him again.

Fieldnotes: McDonald's, Shambles Street

In planning meetings, we often asked where we should meet people (a local guide, a workshop volunteer) and we were invariably told that we should meet 'outside the McDonald's'. After some initial confusion, when looking at Google Maps, and trying to work out where this would be, it turned out that the site of the former McDonald's was actually now a Halifax bank.

This afternoon, as we parted ways briefly, we found ourselves repeating the mistake, 'I'll meet you outside the McDonald's.' It was almost as if we were enacting a kind of time travel, inhabiting a different town from the one we were presently in, one which existed a decade or so ago when the McDonald's had still sat there in the centre of town, the line of taxis waiting just outside it.

At first we caught our own mistakes, correcting ourselves to give the name of the bank, but then decided it might be best to just let it sit, in the hope that it could allow our conversations with the locals we were meeting a smoothness they hadn't had before. We ultimately conclude that after the physical change it takes time for the emotional faculties to catch up. McDonald's no longer exists in that spot, and yet, because we continue to name it, it does. Here we build on the work of Milner and Mace, who talk of the 'gaze as the final brick', that the building only becomes complete when it is known. The Halifax bank is, as yet, incomplete, the money held inside is unreachable. People continue to meet at McDonald's. The town of the mind is not the same as the town of actuality.

And then, amongst the dust and the darkness and the sweat, twenty minutes. The snap tin like a small tugboat; and tea gone lukewarm but not yet cold in the flask. Sitting on the floor, his hands still gritty and oily no matter how many times he wiped them down his legs, and devouring his jam sandwiches, shouting to the others in between stodgy, mucky mouthfuls about whatever the topic of conversation was that day.

The new lads, 'new' regardless of when they started until someone else came up behind them, sitting apart from him and the other older men, eating in silence, occasionally elbowing each other to keep themselves awake.

He shouts over to one of them that he should go to sleep rather than touching himself when he gets in bed, and the men around him cheer. The young lad looks as though he's about to reply but then doesn't, and the men settle again, their talk shifting to other things. Skip's back. Harry's wife. The week in Cleethorpes.

They ask about his heart and he says it's calming down now the winter has passed. He asks about their bodies, their aches; he asks one man how his arm is doing and when the man replies it's much better he asks 'well, why are you still so fucking slow then?' and the men roar with laughter again. The sound of it dull against the walls of their self-made cave.

The crusts where he holds the pieces of bread are thick black by now, so he leaves them. Some of the new ones try chewing their way through, like eating sand. Twenty minutes. Twenty minutes when he reminds himself he has a body, he has a life, there is a world above where they are, and he'll be returning to it.

He drops the crusts back in the tin, and snaps it shut; the hot air is trapped inside so later, when he hands it to her and she unlocks it, there'll be the briefest escape of warmth, like stepping inside on a cold day.

surveillance: CCTV

There were one or two sites which were known as high-traffic spots in the centre because of the number of incidents that occurred there. Shoplifting from the entrances of a couple of shops where cheap items were piled high in bins and there were no security tags on them, making it easy enough to run in and straight back out again. Shop assistants were trained not to tackle the shoplifters, in case things got violent, and so they generally got away with the socks or packs of t-shirts unless one of the security team happened to be around, which meant Ryan and the others try and be around as much as possible. The other spot was the toilets.

They weren't allowed cameras inside but they had two trained on the entrances to the men's and women's and one for the disabled loo, which was down a small cul-de-sac of its own and so was favoured by drug users needing to inject, often meaning it was in use or too unclean for the people who actually needed it.

The men's toilets had a different problem, which often caused giggles or just silence when it was brought up in operational briefings at the start of each morning. The men's toilets on the first floor had, almost since the centre opened but certainly since Ryan had been working there, been known for cottaging. Never anything overtly scandalous, and only once had someone written a letter of complaint to the *Chronicle* about what they'd called 'people up to business they shouldn't be up to in the cubicles'.

Ryan had gone down to try and catch people at it and hadn't ever been able to, though he knew it went on, knew from the furtive glances of the men as they shuffled out, faces down like boys on their way to the headteacher. It was all gesture, a foot under a stall, gently tapping, a hand outstretched at the urinal. If he wasn't working there and if he didn't think he'd get caught, and fired, his dream of a job in the police over before it began, he had to admit there was something alluring about it. Not in the action itself, which always seemed paltry, desolate, but in the theatre of it, the patience it required, the talking without talking.

With the men's toilets it wasn't that you had to watch how people entered, because anyone could stroll in confidently, quickly, as though they were in a rush. You had to watch how people left. They didn't have the slower amble or the half-dance of checking the fly whilst trying to seem like they weren't; the ones who'd been 'up to business they shouldn't be up to in the cubicles' left head-down and straight out of the nearest exit, never any shopping bags, never anyone waiting for them in the mall outside, just straight out onto the street.

As Ryan was surveying the cameras, outside Wilko's, outside Next, outside Primark, he noticed a couple of those kind of men leaving the toilets. He couldn't be bothered, but he thought he should. When he applied to the police he was going to need a good reference and so the next couple of months he was going to really have to get his head down.

He left the control room empty and headed down to the second floor, across the aisle, down the escalator to the first floor. He lingered outside the toilets; not directly outside because that would arouse too much suspicion, but just leaning up against the wall opposite, pretending to be on his phone. One man quickly pushed open the door to the toilets, Ryan looked up from his phone and, as casually as possible, walked in.

Trying to not seem in a rush, and trying not to breathe in through his nose, he walked past the hand dryers and towards the T-junction of the toilet space; to the left the sinks, to the right the child-only area with a lower sink, smaller urinal, and then ahead of him the parallel lines of urinals and toilet cubicles, facing off against each other down each wall. The sinks, Ryan noticed, were free, so too the child's area, and so he kept moving forward.

One young man was finishing up at a urinal, glancing back at Ryan, then leaving quickly, still zipping himself up on the way out, not washing his hands. Ryan pushed each half-open door as he moved down. The two doors down towards the bottom were locked. He could hear heavy breathing.

He made to approach the first locked door but then stopped himself; he didn't really want to see what was going on. He went into the first empty cubicle, put the lid of the toilet down, and sat there for a while. After a minute or so there was a slight tapping on the cubicle wall, so light Ryan almost didn't hear it, and then a black boot, worn rough at the toe curve, came out from under the partition. It tapped twice, and then withdrew itself.

Thirty seconds passed, and then the boot did the same again, followed by the tapping on the partition. Ryan stood up quickly, the automatic sensor behind him setting off the flush. Without looking he banged his fist twice on the locked door, hoped his voice would come out as deep as he wanted it to.

'Come on, lads, think you'd better be moving on.'

He didn't wait for them to come out; he couldn't stand their shame. He just walked back out into the sterile light of the Alhambra, not looking behind at who was following him.

Then back into the dark. Easier for an hour, the food in the furnace of the stomach passing energy to the arms, but then slower again. Telling himself that going slower will only make the rest of the shift feel longer and speeding up, until all the muscles are liquid fire. Until the skin is hot to the touch, and the dust. And the dust. And the dust. Gritty in his sweat, so running a hand over his forehead is like rubbing sand across it. Dark like the bottom of the ocean. The wall high in front of him, as though it might come to break across them all as they dig and split and heave the spoils onto the jittering strip of leather which carries them back out. No light. Just the dust; the occasional rumble in the earth, like it's coughing, as something heavy drives over them, on the surface of things. He thinks there must be some debris and sleck that slides down each time that happens, but how could he know? Just dust into more dust. The wall that never seemed to move, though of course he knew it must do, the walk to the face getting longer, inch by inch, each time they did it, like a tide going out. And he's just treading water, just keeping his head up. Just trying to take a breath, get through the day.

Fieldnotes: Pollyanna

Our work in the town prompts a team member to reminisce about one of its most anomalous paradoxes: Pollyanna, a high-fashion boutique in one of the lowest-paid places in the country. Clothes by Japanese and Scandinavian designers sat in the window of the shop, which looked out onto the grand town hall and a high-end hairdresser's over the road. This is a side of the town which is often overlooked; a study of the most recognisable sites to outsiders would potentially include the football ground, the old pit wheel so often in the background of news stories, and perhaps the outdoor markets. These are the familiar. Pollyanna is the strange. A few years ago, the member of our team came across a crocodile-skin belt in the shop, housed in a glass case up the stairs and to the left, just next to the banister. She asked if it was real and a thin sales assistant dressed all in black told her that it was. It retailed at £800.

Sometimes Pollyanna used to close to the public and celebrities were given private tours of the collections. It felt out of place, but also like something which spun outward from the insularity we so often encountered within the different research spaces in the town. It offered the potential for escape. A portal to elsewhere. It closed in 2014. It is a cake shop now.

Later that evening, after hours of being shouted at down the phone, Simon sat framed by the mucky mirror on the wall. Downstairs the music rose suddenly, vibrating beneath the dark grey carpet, and then dropped, before rising again. They were testing the sound, making sure it was all ready for opening time. They'd open at eight, and his first tour of duty on the stage would be at nine. Just the usual: welcoming people, the same old jokes the regulars still had the courtesy to laugh at. He'd use that time to scan the room, check for any trouble-makers, make a plan for who to try and get up on stage. He'd spot the young students he could bring up willingly, who weren't too shy, who'd join in the dance routines later on. Then he'd come off, have a couple of quick shots, and then on again, to lip-synch to the club favourites. They wouldn't be his choices, but they were popular, and the manager just wanted the punters to be happy. When they were happy they bought more drinks.

He started with the eyebrows, always. Covering them in quick circular motions with a gluestick. His had always been quite thick, not quite joining in the middle but close, something the kids in school had always pointed out to him. Since doing drag, he'd kept them thinner, further apart, but still every time he looked at himself in the mirror as they began to disappear, he saw the odd hill of his head as if for the first time, and was quietly disgusted by himself. Then he brushed the glue, working out any lumps or creases, getting it as close to his skin and as even as possible, and dabbed at any excess with a wipe. Below him, the music swelled and fell away in waves. It was so routine to him now that he could lose himself in it, allow his mind to wander to Ryan, who he hadn't spoken to in two days, which he knew wasn't long at all really, in the grand scheme of things, but felt historic in the rushed month where they'd been in each other's phone every minute and in each other's bed most nights.

His foundation was darker than his own skin, but only slightly. The brush was one he'd had for years, since he first started, before he knew all about the different types and what they might do or what different design features they might have. He'd picked it out of the plastic tubs they kept the bargains in at the front of the pharmacy, and even though the bristles were loosening, all blown out like an exploded dandelion clock, he liked the familiar feel of it in his hand. He did the base first, around the edges, setting the borders of his new face, and then a lighter colour under the eyes, at the sides of the nose, the recess above his top lip, and his chin.

Next it was the sponge, faded from all the shows and all the faces he'd put on, and he blended the lighter and darker foundation together. And then the contour lines, the architecture of the new face, bringing the angles out. The eyeshadow, something that would really pop for the drunks at the back of the room, and the eyelashes, sticking on one false pair and then another pair over them, so there was a three-dimensional effect that seemed to make the eyes a deep well to peer down into. And then it was the wig, styled and fluffed on a Styrofoam mannequin they'd once been throwing out from the college, and glued down beneath the line of the hair cap, fastened into place with bobby pins. He closed his eyes, as tight as he could, what with the lashes, and sprayed the whole thing with hairspray, to hold it in place against the sweat. He put on the glittery thigh-skimming dress that caught the light and sent it shattering back out onto the dancefloor; the same one he'd worn last Sunday, because he knew it would be a different crowd for the different day of the week.

Last, he shook his head to check the wig wouldn't come off. It had happened to another queen at a club in Rotherham and the video had gone viral, the butt of a million different jokes, punchlines to things she'd had nothing to do with. He lived in fear of that happening to him. So the shaking to make sure, and the looking in the mirror to check every angle was just right. He put his phone on charge, because this was a dressing room that locked so it was safe, checking it one last time to see if there was anything from Ryan. There wasn't. Simon looked at himself one last time in the mirror, and stepped out as Puttana Short Dress.

The phone was in Ryan's hand, and then face down on the bed, and then in his hand again. He still had the shirt on from work but untucked, unbuttoned down to the waist. Simon's OnlyFans profile, the link to which he'd sent over to Ryan with one of those emojis of a monkey covering its face after that first meeting, was on the screen, his username, BarnsleyLad28, displayed at the top. There was a price for new subscribers: $8.99 a month.

When Simon had first sent it over to Ryan, he'd understood it as some sort of shorthand, not bothering with days or weeks of teased nudes and endless flirtation, no slow dismantling of walls, but a baring of everything, straight away.

To sign up, Ryan had had to make his own profile. He'd wanted to remain anonymous, scared that putting in something even close to his real name would jeopardise his chances with the police. He'd gone with CopperPipe, and had to put his postcode in, which disconcerted him, as though the neighbours might all be simultaneously alerted that someone in the back bedroom of the house up the road had signed up to a website to view questionable content.

This time, as each time since, Ryan's entrance to the page was smoother, his phone remembering the link, nudging him when he was only halfway through it. And then there Simon was. Little squares of Simon. Simon topless, his slim tight frame angled down at the camera, Simon in his underwear, sitting on the bed, the camera looking up at him from the floor, Simon in a tracksuit, Simon with nothing on, laying with his legs spread on the bed. Further down there was Simon in a dress, Simon in lingerie, each one with a grey circle and a white arrow asking him to press play, to bring these various Simons to life.

The videos and images were arranged by date, and Ryan recognised the more recent ones, but if you clicked on the right-hand corner you could arrange by number of views, or the ones that had garnered the highest number of tips. The one that was most popular with subscribers was the one that Ryan remembered watching that first time. Someone else was in the square and it wasn't Simon. The legs were too broad, the chest too hairy. The figure in the frame was cut off at the neck, so their head wasn't visible. Ryan would have guessed someone in their mid-thirties, no visible tattoos. The video was called 'surprising a friend'. The headless figure stroked himself, and the way the light seemed to change and modulate on his body suggested he was watching something on screen. After thirty seconds or so he pulled down the front of his boxers and held his dick in his hand. He kept stroking. The light that played across his body kept changing in brightness and intensity. The door opened. The body at the centre of the screen turned to look, and then went back to the TV. It was Simon at the door. Dressed in Adidas tracksuit bottoms and a coat, as though he was just getting home from the gym.

Ryan's gaze was interrupted by a text notification coming through at the top of the screen, and he clicked on it without reading who it was from, assuming it would be Simon, but it was just his boss, asking if he could pick up another shift. When Ryan flicked back to the video, it started buffering, as though punishing him for lack of attention. The clip kept jumping, Simon arriving into the room over and over again, the circle turning over the space where the man's head should have been.

Ryan went back to his text messages, sent a thumbs-up to his boss, and then clicked through to Simon's messages. Nothing since Sunday, since the heart-eyed face Simon had sent when Ryan had messaged him to tell him he was at the club. Ryan started to type, but the words wouldn't come. He let himself lie in the glare of the screen for a while, and then put the phone face down on the bed again.

Despite his lamp and the lights rigged up above him, it's dark work. And hot. Hotter than any day of summer would ever get on the surface. Working permanently in the night, sweating, the coal dust on his wet hands, across his wet forehead, turning into a paste, into paint that smears down his shorts and his bare chest. And the smell; the feral undergrowth of men mixing with the soot, the oil of the belt. Like being trapped and trying to dig yourself out. Always checking the ceiling just in case, stopping every twenty minutes to check everything was stable. And then back to the digging, or the hacking or the lifting, shovelling it onto the belt, sometimes pieces the size of a fist, sometimes the size of a head, sometimes just shovel-fuls of sleck and rocks. Onto the belt. Watching them vanish into the dark. And the dust. The dust that settles inside him, the way dust settles in a museum. Men turning into museums of themselves. And the dust. And the dust. And sometimes a breeze from the ventilation but most of the time just like being inside an oven. The weight of the world on top of him, and the depths of everything underneath him. And the dust, settling and rising on him, every time he takes a breath.

The music below was a dull thud, but still enough to make the glass and the make-up bag agitate on the table. Simon looked at himself through the dust on the mirror. The wig and the make-up had just about survived.

He peeled the eyelashes off first, each curl almost longer than his little finger, and pressed them neatly back into the padded pencil case he used to carry them; they'd still be good for another couple of times. Next it was the hair, which always hurt, no matter how gently he did it. The thick line of glue, that ran in grey around the circumference of his skull, making him look like a monk.

Downstairs, he could hear people singing along to one of the ones the DJ put on when he wanted to slip outside for some air and needed something reliable to make sure that nobody noticed.

The show had gone OK tonight; nobody had really been paying attention, which Simon preferred. They were a young crowd, and an almost even split between straight and gay.

One time someone had thrown a glass and it had shattered just to the right of him, but he'd kept on dancing and slowly managed to shuffle the glass over the edge.

One time two drunk students jumped on stage and started dancing and wouldn't get off and so Simon had just left them to it, and it seemed as though the crowd didn't even notice.

One time he'd been doing a cabaret routine which ended with some young innocent in their boxer shorts on a chair as Simon straddled him, singing. This time someone had run on stage, screaming, and thrown a drink in the kid's face. Simon's miming did not miss a beat.

One time a hen party was in, and one of the women had grabbed him by the crotch, was confused momentarily by the lack in what she found, and then slapped him. He'd left that night and didn't go back for three weeks until the manager rang and offered to give him sixty-five instead of the usual fifty pounds. That meant sixty more a month, which covered the train every week. 'It'll pay for some-thing,' his dad had said. That, plus the three hundred and ten he got from the call centre each week, plus the bits from OnlyFans, which fluctuated but maybe a hundred, a hundred and fifty dollars, meant that he could get by OK. Pay the rent on the flat, the bills, his phone, try and make more than the minimum on the credit card he'd maxed out when he was first buying costumes.

There'd been one night at home, before his mum'd left, he'd come downstairs and seen her hunched over the table, phone open on the calculator, scribbling on the back of an envelope. She'd seen him, beckoned him over to her. 'They won't teach you this in school,' she'd said, and gone through how she budgeted for the week, what things cost. 'Always try and have a separate account for the bills,' she'd said, 'that way whatever's left you know's yours to spend how you want. You don't want to be owing nothing to anybody, if you can help it.' So he still did that, and each month, those couple of days before payday, he'd shuffle between the two cards, seeing which one was a bit less overdrawn, which one could stand a takeaway coffee, a round at the pub. The last day of the month it would get replenished, and then the next day it would be the electric, or the TV licence, or Netflix, or the gym hacking away at the digits, making them smaller. Somehow his mum was always in the back of his mind when it came to his money, feeling she might be pleased with him as he divvied up his bills the way she'd said, feeling the weight of her disappointment whenever he logged in to the Mastercard app.

He did the make-up next, wiping it off in thick scoops, like an excavation, digging back to himself, layers of foundation and concealer and sweat and the sticky moisture of the bar. It always took longer than he remembered it doing, no matter how many times a week he did it. That's why, depending how brave he was feeling, or rather how much he thought he could stand being looked at, he'd leave the eye make-up on, or some of the foundation, sort it out when he got home, anxious not to miss the last train. That's what Ryan hadn't liked.

Simon had told him about the drag straight away, and the OnlyFans, because there'd been times in the past when one or the other or sometimes both had put people off. Last Sunday he'd finally persuaded him to come; Ryan was nervous about coming to see Simon's show at the club, in front of people he might know, and so Simon had said for him to come to Sheffield instead. He could be anonymous there. Simon couldn't really believe that Ryan had never been to a drag show before, there were plenty of queens who worked the once-a-week gay night in town, but Ryan had said not, it had never really been his thing.

That Sunday, when Simon stepped onto the stage, he'd seen Ryan sitting towards the back of the room; Ryan had put his pint down and had done an exaggerated wave over to the front of the room and Simon, now in character as Puttana, did an exaggerated coquettish wink back to him, and then went into the number. It was a fast one, and Simon's mind had been taken up with thinking about the next line, the next move he had to push his body into performing, so he forgot about being watched by Ryan.

It had been surprisingly busy for a Sunday, for which Simon was glad; he hadn't wanted Ryan seeing the club half empty, spaces and sticky stains on the floor in between small groups of people. When Simon finished the song people cheered enthusiastically, and he'd got to do a comedy bit he hadn't done in months where he went off and kept coming back on and then fetched his own flowers out in an exaggerated encore routine. When it was winding down, he stopped coming back out and the DJ took that as his cue to start the music up. They had an all-evening happy hour on a Sunday, so it would just be dance music from now on; it would be pointless trying to get people to focus on the stage any more. It was just best to let them move, let them throw their lust into each other on the dancefloor until they left, arms around different people than they'd arrived with.

Simon had texted Ryan and told him that he'd be out soon and Ryan had texted back *no worries*. He wanted to just get out, to see what Ryan had made of it all, to go home with him. The last train on a Sunday left earlier, before eleven, and so he'd rushed getting ready, slipping on his skinny jeans, vest, a plaid shirt over the top. He stuffed his costume without folding into his bag, knowing he'd regret it in a couple of days when it was time to perform again. Looking in the mirror, he'd peeled off the eyelashes, wiped some of the make-up, but left some of it around his eyes to speed things up. When he'd approached Ryan at the bar he'd downed his pint, his second, maybe even third, and they'd kissed briefly on the lips, Ryan saying 'oh, here she is'.

He'd looked Simon up and down, not unkindly, and then said 'You've missed some of the makeup, Si. Do you wanna go and wipe it up and then we can get going?' Simon had already been moving towards the door, saying 'Oh no, it's fine, I'll just sort it out when we get home.'

Ryan would deny it as they argued on the way to the station, but Simon swore he saw him flinch slightly. Simon had walked back towards him. 'It's OK, nobody's going to say anything, you know. And even if they did, you'll protect me, won't you?' He'd slipped back into Puttana for that last phrase, acting a damsel in distress. Ryan hadn't replied, just picked his jacket up and walked by Simon towards the door.

Simon couldn't remember, now, what had been said, on that walk to the train station, and knew for certain barely anything had been said on the journey itself as they pulled out of the city: Chapeltown, Elsecar, Wombwell. The recorded announcement always emphasised *womb* as the platform approached, enunciating both syllables so the place sounded alien to Simon, not the *Wumwell* he was used to hearing and saying. He'd wanted so much for Ryan to see him, to leave with him, to be seen with him. On stage, Simon had to make himself bigger to hold the room, keep their attention else it slip away like water. But afterwards, as he headed for the last train back home, he always felt lower, stuck to the floor in his trainers after the exaggeration of heels.

That Sunday, just like tonight, the train was quiet, some workers slumped out and sleeping in their hi-vis vests and their paint-stained jeans. Sometimes drunk couples, falling over each other asleep and stumbling off as the brakes screamed their arrival into each station. Ryan's silence had hardened that night, with each passing minute. Simon had just curled up in a two-seater, made himself small, let the night wash over him as the train bore him home.

He steps out into the long corridor of early dawn; the street rolling on endlessly, like a runaway train. Above, the sky is a dark chimney, and three doors down Pat is just closing his front door. Another few doors on there will be Harry and then Frank, and as they all turn the corner together Skip will already be ahead of them, and Frank will run to catch up to finish their debate from yesterday. Nobody speaks; they incline their heads as someone else joins them and then keep on walking. More and more men fall out of their houses, some smiling slightly, the week already on the downward slope. Occasionally some stop, and lean for a moment on the low wall of a garden, pretending to re-tie their boot, hawking up yesterday's shift from their lungs as they crouch down. Nobody waits for them, they just keep on walking. The village, on their shoulder now, still asleep, not watching the migration of tired bodies. One of the men once said he thought he could hear the coal laughing. Another man told him to stop talking daft. And beneath their feet, a mile down, ancient trees, forced smaller by millennia of pressure, waiting to be brought back out into the sun.

That Sunday evening, after the silent train ride home, Ryan had stayed at Simon's, leaving early to get ready for his shift at the shopping centre. They'd had sex but only after Simon had washed his face and got rid of the last remaining traces of Puttana. Ryan hadn't asked but he hadn't really needed to, and then, as now this Wednesday morning, Simon woke up in his flat alone, and went to the bathroom, balling up the wipes and folding the cotton pads into themselves to put in a half-empty cup of cold tea and take them to the kitchen.

His face in the harsh bathroom light looked tired, and because it looked tired it looked drawn and so even thinner than usual. It had taken a long time for Simon to stop equating that with something to celebrate, to decide that he didn't just want to be skin and bones. As a child he'd always been overweight. The other kids in school hadn't let him forget it, though they didn't know the half of it,

Simon now realised: that he had to wear jogging bottoms or trousers taken up at the ankle by inches and inches because they had to be adult-sized in order to go around his waist. The first time he'd ever heard the word gay was when someone called it him in school, in that generically insulting way, but it seemed to Simon now that maybe they knew, that kids are just very perceptive when it comes to figuring things out about each other. They'd called him things that don't get said any more, not because of tolerance or anything like that, but because insults like anything else move in and out of fashion. Some of the things just seem so silly now that it's weird they ever could have hurt so much. *Puff. Batty boy. Knob jockey. Sausage jockey.* They'd been said as regularly, as easily, as his own name. But he'd only ever been hit once. Waiting for the 219 bus, when a young boy, maybe thirteen when Simon had been fifteen, had wandered over and without speaking just punched him in the face before walking back to his mates, laughing.

School had felt like an endless stream of things designed to catch him out. Asking him who he fancied. If he'd ever snogged a girl. One game where some lad would ask if he had hair 'on his dick', to which there was no right answer because if you said no they'd tease you over being 'pube-less' but if you said yes they'd laugh hysterically and say you had hair on your dick instead of your balls and so must be some sort of freak. Everything always felt like it was happening for him on a slightly different frequency to his classmates. Three p.m. when the lessons ended and he walked home felt like finally being able to breathe, to take in fresh air, to have survived another day. Afterwards, even when he started working in the club, the word gay would ring in the pit of his stomach, a pang of worry, the word dropping like a stone and echoing out from all the years of before.

When Ryan had looked at him, with what felt like disgust, he'd suddenly felt conspicuous again. Not visible as Puttana, but visible as himself; not a voice down a phone that someone called to place a bet, not a well-lit fantasy for someone to wank to, not a brassy, confident drag queen, just Simon, looking too gay to be seen with. He didn't know how to explain that to Ryan, that to be looked at, and who was looking, were these complex turning cogs that lifted panic up into his mind or sunk shame deep down inside him. Somehow, Simon thought, for Ryan to be seen with him while he was still wearing make-up – and not even that much make-up, thought Simon bitterly, as he swilled the dregs of the tea down the sink – would mean that he was seen as well, in a different light, some reflection from Simon hitting Ryan, causing everyone to turn and look.

Simon grabbed his phone, pushed his thumb over Ryan's name and texted: *are you embarrassed by me?*

surveillance: gossip

After Simon and Ryan had left that Sunday evening, one of the two younger queens whose job it was to work the door, pull people flirtily in off the street, or else walk around selling shots, was saying, as she removed her wig, that guy who was here with Simon, honestly, proper barged me as he left, and then Simon, he's always been all right with me since I started, always thought he probably fancied me like. What? Don't look at me like that, I'm sure he fancied you n'all, but he just waltzes on past, doesn't he, like he's Queen of Sheba, did you see him though when Simon was on stage, just sitting at the back like, kept looking at his phone, wasn't really paying attention, well all right yeah he was looking over at the stage but you could tell in his eyes, I went over with a shot, and just this glazed look like, and then Simon comes out and he's still got that eye make-up on and I've tried to say I'll help him blend it better like, sent him a link to one of my tutorials but he weren't having it, anyway Simon is looking all happy and the other bloke's there and he is fit to be fair, right? Those arms? Anyway, clearly something goes on, and I can't hear really what it is but I felt like they could tell I was earwigging and that's when I grabbed you and pulled you outside 'cos I thought they might carry on a bit once they'd left but it was something to do with the make-up, the bloke didn't look happy that Simon wouldn't take it off like, I mean who gives a fuck, he's just been dancing around in a dress and now he's worried about a little bit of make-up but it's like I said about that guy I was dating, isn't it, they always want it to be one way or the other, not in-between. So it's either like you're dead femme all the time, and they love that, or you leave all the drag stuff as soon as you leave the club and you're just like one of the lads for them, it's always either/or, so Simon comes down with a bit of make-up. Makes it messy, blurs it for him, it's not just one thing or another any more, is it?

The other queen looked up briefly and smiled in agreement, then went back to his phone, pushing the button on an app that called a cab to his precise location.

When Brian had gone back for the next session he'd been the only one, aside from the woman from the food bank, who kept anxiously checking the door. The men, the younger one and the older one, from the university, kept smiling, saying it was fine, they knew how busy people were, that they all had lives, that probably something had come up. Brian didn't say anything, just let their words fall across the tables they'd shoved back together in the middle of the club. They still had his cards; they were a little dog-eared, and the younger one of them had to brush off crumbs as he pulled them from his bag, but he had to admit that he felt a little happiness at seeing them, squashed in tight together with a rubber band. The younger one passed them to him, and asked if he wouldn't mind arranging them on the table, if he could remember where they'd been before. 'If I can remember,' he parroted back, tutting, 'of course I can remember, it's my life, isn't it? Just let me get a tea first, before it stews.' The younger one looked taken aback but as he went over to the urn Brian winked at the older one and flashed a quick smile to the woman, to try and show that he'd only been teasing.

As he began to spread the cards out on the table, he was struck by the silence in the club; without the other couple of them there was nobody to keep up the low hum of conversation. He'd chosen a seat at the far end of the table, and the two men from the university had sat at the other end, and so it felt like he was at some sort of job interview, or sanctions meeting, a long expanse unrolling between them. He couldn't stand the quiet. He asked them what they'd been up to, and though they seemed surprised at first to be included in a conversation, exchanging that glance between the two of them that he'd noticed last time, they seemed excited at the prospect. 'Erm, teaching mainly,' the younger one said. 'What do you teach?' he'd asked. 'English,' the younger one had said. 'I know that,' he said, 'you told me that last time, honestly you think I've got Alzheimer's, you. I mean what bit of English. Like, books?' His tone flustered the young one again, though the older one of the two tried to smile, as though he was in on the joke. 'My area of expertise is linguistics, I suppose really, and spelling, so at the moment I'm thinking about the inherent power structures of non-standard English in written communications.' Brian asked him to explain what that meant, in English this time, lad, and the younger one said 'Well, we all have an accent, for example, and if you were to write something down how you'd pronounce it, some people might say that's not "correct", but it's correct to you because that's how you'd say the word, and how a lot of people who you speak to every day might say the word as well.'

'What about jobs, though?' Brian asked. The younger one hadn't replied but the older one had made eye contact in a way that seemed to suggest he should continue. 'Well, if someone is with the work coach and he asks them to fill a form in and they just spell things how they say them, what job is going to take them seriously?' 'Well, that's the point,' the younger one said, 'maybe we could help to change their mind.'

'How long would that take?' he'd asked. 'They'd have found someone else to do that job before you'd even started.'

And the heat and the heat and the dust and the sleck and the shallow breath and the sleck from the roof and the spit on the floor and the sweat and grit on their arms, on their legs, and the muck and the dust and the dust and the dust and the dust and the heat and the heat from the lamp and the heat of the breath that rattles like a coin in a tin, and the noise, and the muck and the dust and the dust and the dust and the dust and the heat and the coughs and the arm across the brow and the arm above the head, in front of the face and the splitting and the breaking and the pulling and the heaving and the drill and the belt and its churn and the heat and the grit in the air and the sleck from the lungs and the spit on the floor and the dust and the dust and the dust and the dust and the dust and the dust and all the world above him, like a dream.

Sometimes, when Alex is at home, sitting on his settee, this is what he remembers. The time in the bar when he was too drunk to stand, holding himself up against the wall near the DJ booth, a man shouting whatthefuckdoyouthink-you'relookingat, a man shouting fuckingweirdostaring, a fist. And her face when he got home, assuming another pissed-up fight. Sometimes anger, sometimes the thin plywood of the bedroom door closing on his blurred vision as he propped himself up on the banister, and sometimes there were wet eyes, on the edge of tears.

Sometimes, when he closes his eyes, he can hear her saying 'You can just tell me, you know, you don't need to keep lying,' and sometimes it's just a feeling that comes over him, that anxiety that drink always drags behind itself into the next morning, a fear of having slipped up, that some-where in the dark tunnel of the things you can't remember, everyone was watching you, and their eyes are still on you, like a warning.

Simon's text had come through, and Ryan had felt the relief of contact after the silence, like breaking through a wall, and then the shame of not having been the one to text first. They'd agreed to meet at the club later, and now Ryan sat, a cup of coffee and an unopen textbook about the 1984 Police and Criminal Evidence Act in front of him, his laptop warm and whirring on his thigh. When Simon had asked him directly, about whether he was embarrassed by him, he hadn't known what to say. He wasn't. He didn't think he was. Not consciously. It was just something about Simon's make-up and who he was when he wore it that made sense to Ryan inside a club but not outside of one.

On the screen, Ryan minimised a document he'd headed *notes* and moved his cursor idly round the screen. The icon for solitaire, his emails, old photos that he'd scanned at some point but not got around to organising. He stopped over a file marked *uploads*. He didn't click onto it; he didn't need to. It was where he'd stored a couple of films for Simon's page, the raw footage, and then the version with the little bits of editing he'd promised to do. There were moments, passing time before getting up for work, unable to sleep and Simon already snoring beside him, that he'd go in and watch older clips, from before they'd met. The newer ones, the couple he'd co-starred in, he didn't need to watch; they played vivid as a cinema screen in his mind.

The first time he'd agreed to it, there were two cameras set up in the room. One had just been Simon's mobile phone, propped up against a lamp and facing the bed, framing it like a landscape. The other had been on a tripod, at the head of the bed, portrait, and face-on to the action.

In the raw footage, that Ryan had watched in a kind of daze afterwards, you could see Simon bending down in front of each camera, extending a finger towards the screen that gradually became larger and more blurred. Topless as he bent over, the flat thinness of his chest, the valley of his collarbone. There was sound too, that Simon had asked him to edit out when the video was uploaded, and which Ryan had replaced with a slowed down version of a house music classic. In the raw cut, the camera and the phone both picked up Ryan saying 'Are you sure, though, they won't see my face?' and Simon reassuring him that no they wouldn't, it would cut off at his neck and it wasn't like he had any tattoos or anything that made him recognisable and he just had to think really, anyone he was worried about seeing him do something like this was hardly likely to be the sort of person that was watching it. 'It's because of the police, the tattoos,' Ryan had said. Simon said he knew and they didn't have to do it if he really didn't want to, but nobody would ever know it was him, most of the subscribers were in America anyway, or Eastern Europe, or London, it wasn't like he was going to bump into someone on the street who was suddenly going to tell everyone. 'I'm not ashamed,' Ryan had told him, the audio picking up the sharpness in his voice, 'it's just some things are meant to be private.' 'Don't you find it a little bit hot, though, having an audience,' Simon had asked, 'like someone is looking through the window while you're with me and you're showing off, you're performing.' 'I mean, yeah, I guess,' Ryan had heard himself admitting. 'Even when I'm filming just myself,' Simon had told him, 'it's the idea of the private being public, or something about exhibitionism, everyone can see me, and they're here because they want to be, because I've got something they want, but it's just the other end of a phone camera, so they can't have it, and that frustration, it's so similar to lust, and that's what keeps them watching.' 'Fucking hell,' Ryan had laughed, 'was all that from a presentation before you signed up or something?'

The mobile phone camera had shown Simon leading Ryan around to the near side of the bed, Simon standing with his back to the screen; the sound of buttons being undone, of a shirt being wrestled off two arms, of Ryan's stocky frame falling back onto the bed, lengthways across it. Then

Simon bending down, pulling at his slim-fit jeans from the bottom of the leg, off with one and then the other, until the back of his plain black briefs is all the viewers can see. 'Shuffle back a bit,' Simon could be heard saying, 'and then if you hang your head off the side, that other camera will just get you from the neck down.' 'What about that one?' Ryan had asked, of the phone behind Simon. 'That'll just get me,' Simon replied.

Later, when the video had been uploaded, it was under the headline 'servicing a mate'. Subscribers got to see Simon, still in the briefs, begin on his knees in front of the bed, just the crown of his head visible in front of a body that appears from one angle to be all legs. It's this shot, the phone one, that the subscribers started with, Simon turning to look at them and then back to the legs, his tongue starting in small licks from the shin, into longer trails up the thighs and to the bulge in the loose boxers the body is wearing. They got to see Simon grab the bulge, turn around to the camera again and open his mouth slightly, as though in shock, before returning his tongue to the boxers, circling the crotch with wet licks, like he's trying to unfasten the three white plastic buttons on the front. Subscribers then got the different view, the camera one, Simon suddenly in profile as he looks over to them again, like he's unsure they'll still be there. Simon slowly moving his hand up the bare torso that the frame cuts off at the neck, fingers occasionally wrapping themselves around the slight matting of body hair, or squeezing the chest hard. No sound from the other person, just a slight shift in intensity of the backing music, and then Simon, without breaking eye contact with the camera, slowly pulling the boxers down, and taking the whole of what's revealed in his mouth. Subscribers still got the eye contact, Simon staring right down the barrel of the camera lens as his head moves up and down the shaft. He never touches himself, never brings his own body too close to the one he is pleasuring. The shot is framed perfectly, Simon bending down from a kneeling position, his knees between the two thicker, hairier legs. Subscribers occasionally got a cut away to the phone footage, which suddenly seems grainier, more DIY by comparison, as though someone is in the room with them, filming, and just Simon's bum is visible, his head occasionally as it bobs up and down. Then back to the camera, Simon's hand running the length of the body in front of him, speeding up, his other hand at the base of the shaft, until there's a tremor in the body and the subscribers got to see the pulse of his throat as he swallows, then licks his lips, then smiles at the camera. The music getting louder as the picture fades away, and the title comes back onto the screen.

In the raw footage, Simon says to Ryan that he can come up now, and he does, shuffling himself onto the bed, his face red from the encounter and the blood rushing to his head from where it had been held for so long. You can see Simon shuffle over his body slightly, so his knees are either side of Ryan's torso. His hands over each of his pecs. 'Who did you imagine was watching?' Simon asks, the hint of a smile visible. 'Everyone,' Ryan replies, still trying to catch his breath.

Fieldnotes: Trauma

At the end of the last decade, Dr Geoff Bright built on the thinking in Dr Avery Gordon's *Ghostly Matters: Haunting and the Sociological Imagination*. The work of Bright developed the idea of a Social Haunting, and brought it to bear on post-industrial landscapes, in which he was drawing on Beverley Skeggs to develop an approach that centred 'person value and autonomist working-class value practices'. Bright himself has written:

According to Gordon, a social haunting is an entangling reminder of lingering trouble relating to 'social violence done in the past' and a notification 'that what's been concealed is very much alive and present' (1997: xvi.). While the general idea that the past remains present *in* the present is nothing new in the scholarship referred to above, the specific notion of a social haunting does break new ground.

Social ghosts, Gordon emphasises, while strongly *felt* are *not easily known*, as the evidence of their existence is 'often *barely visible or highly symbolised*'.

We hold these words in our head each morning as we drive through the town, and the villages at its outskirts. The social violence done in the past is the obvious one. What is concealed, beneath the ground, still very much alive and present, still breathing, still prone to cough, to slippage, to subsidence.

'The past remains present *in* the present'. That evening, we watch a national television news report on regional inequality, where a suited reporter stands in front of the decommissioned pit head, which still sits on the shoulder of the town.

We pose some questions to each other, to our fellow academics reading this article, as we acknowledge our debt to Bright, to Gordon, to Skeggs: what is it that is being concealed? What does it mean for it to be alive and present? What is it to be looked at, but not seen? What is the difference between feeling and knowing? Why does the news reporter always choose to stand where he stands?

After another couple of teas, and a plate of sandwiches excessive for the number of people in the room, Brian finished the task he'd been set. They'd asked him to lay out the cards as he had last time, then given him another set and this time asked if he'd cover up the cards of the 'past' with what was there now. Where he'd put the corner shop, what was there now, they'd asked him. 'Nothing,' he'd replied, and so they'd told him to write nothing on the card and put it over the top. He'd gone on like that. A couple of people still lived where they always had, but a lot of places he either hadn't visited in years, or were gone entirely. The Rec was a new housing estate, called Storm, the school was just fields now, and a couple of locals let their horses graze on them to keep the grass down. The Old Bridge was still the Old Bridge, but they'd painted it. Mr Mawi's shop was a Co-op, and he'd drawn three pound signs on the card to show what that had done to the price of the fruit in there.

Again, it seemed to him that they were interested in the strangest things. Across where before he'd just written *pit fields*, he'd written *The New Road*, and then drawn an arrow across several cards to show how it pulled around the edges of the village and then off to the ends of the tables (towards the motorway). They'd wanted to know a lot more about this New Road. They'd asked him when it had been built, and though he didn't know exactly, he could still remember the different planning meetings they'd held, the letters in the *Chronicle* arguing about it. He guessed it had been built in around '95/'96.

'That's almost a quarter of a century ago,' the older one of them had said. 'Interesting that it's still the New Road, isn't it?'

He'd shrugged, it was just the name of it, and it was a very good example of something which wasn't at all interesting to him but seemed to fascinate them. He told them it had been controversial at the time, that a lot of people had wanted to keep the fields, that they were popular for families going walking. They'd asked him how he'd felt about it. He'd shrugged again. He couldn't remember, not really, and certainly he'd never felt strongly enough about it one way or another, never wrote letters or signed any of the petitions. There'd even been one man, he said, who came door to door asking for signatures.

'But you never got involved with any of that?' they'd asked again.

He'd said not, he'd said that, in fairness, in his opinion, roads needed to go somewhere, and they called this one a bypass, and that literally means taking things away, taking things out of somewhere, right? 'I guess I thought villages like ours had had enough of that,' Brian said.

They liked that a lot, and went back to their notepads.

The suit was something Simon had managed to find at a charity shop. It was almost perfect; not quite an exact replica but striking enough of the right notes that it would start the films playing in people's minds. The blue two-piece; his was single-breasted, though mostly she'd worn double-breasted, but that was the kind of detail he felt that people would be able to forgive. The broadness of his shoulders meant the blazer finished a little way above his navel, and he'd debated whether that meant he should go with a shirt underneath, but he liked the flash of skin, the smooth pale light of his flesh shining out. The skirt was longer, much longer than he'd usually wear to do drag in, and concertinaed in the way a napkin might be at a posh restaurant. He was conscious, though, that this shouldn't be a re-enactment, it should be drag, and so he cut out holes on the back to make it look almost like chaps. And then the shoes; he'd found a cheap pair of court shoes in a bargain bin at Wynsors, the sort that offered a slight lift in height, but they hadn't felt right, and when he'd tried to move around the room they'd been too solid, too weighty, holding him down to the ground. He'd asked his dad if he could take a photograph of his old pit boots, of grandad's old pit boots, and his dad had been confused but said yes and so, armed with some paint, and a scouring pad to scratch away at the fresh-dried layers, he'd gone about fashioning a pair of Uggs into something that resembled manual workwear. They'd be comfy, and mean he could move around and dance, but they'd look sturdy, give an illusion of strength.

The hair he'd had ready for a long time, occasionally returning to make sure each strand was exactly in place, so it was just the little things, a string of pearls (plastic, from Claire's), the sensible, thin strap of a watch. He'd painted an old document holder red to look like one of the red boxes ministers carried around to look important. He wasn't Her, but he was a version of her. Maggie come back, Maggie returned, Maggie exposed, Maggie on show, and both of them perhaps seen for the first time for who they really were.

*Walking through the ginnel of the two houses over the road leads
into the allotment. On the top, the grass trodden down into mud is
the path he walks along, before turning left and down the old concrete
blocks onto his plot of land. He surveys it; the thin tunnels of earth
dug with carrots, cabbages, potatoes. He breathes in, the smell of the
soil, the smell of the chickens from two plots over, the muck they've
been spreading on the fields over the way. He breathes out, and
there's gravel in his chest. He sits on the old dining-room chair he'd
found at the end of the street one morning, and looks at how things
are doing. Some evenings, like this one, there wasn't any work to
be done. Sometimes the spade and the hand-turned rotary plough
and the watering can stayed in the tumbledown shed. An allotment
patch didn't have to be neat, not the way she wanted the front
garden. He didn't weed. He didn't sweep the dust from the steps.
Evenings like this one, just sitting, the large sky beyond the roofs.*

*At some point, who knows after how long, he stands, spitting the
mulch up from his lungs to the side of the chair leg, and walks*

to the far end of his oblong of land. He walks over to the only thing down there. The racing pigeons in their large wooden coop. Mainly grey ones, with a few white ones he'd been given by a mate just before he'd died, each one with its own little box to perch in against the walls. He wouldn't do it now, because it was too late, and anyway the atmosphere hadn't been right all day, the wind coming in from the wrong direction. Another time, though, next time he was here, he'd reach in, not just to where he scattered the food, but reach in to one of them, cupping it like water in his hands, and he'd lift it out of the dark of where it lived, and he'd lift it up, and he'd throw it gently, and that's all it would need to be up and off, beyond the chimneys. And he'd go and sit back down, and wait for whatever instinct was bred into it to kick in, and for it to come home.

In the afternoon a poet had arrived, and a couple of the men from the first session had sloped in as well. It felt to Brian like maybe they were already running out of ideas, circling around the same few miles of conversation, so they had to try and mix it up, throw a curve ball.

The poet was young, had an accent that seemed as though it had begun here but flowered elsewhere – familiar and yet not at the same time. He'd placed an old mug that had come from an Easter egg in the middle of the table, filled with pens, and some scraps of plain and lined paper piled up beside it.

'Right!' said the poet to them all, and the way he said that word, slightly too high-pitched, slightly too loud, told Brian he was nervous. He felt bad for the lad, he must only be Simon's age, and the way he'd said 'right', not 'reight', still that drawn out long vowel, but a different sound, less clumpy somehow, less local. He had tattoos like old sailors have up and down his arms, despite looking far too young to ever have been to sea. They were told to think of a famous landmark in the town – either one that was still there, 'like the town hall', the poet suggested, or one which used to be there but wasn't any more, 'like the bandstand'. The same things, thought Brian, the same questions, being asked over and over again just in different ways. 'Once you've chosen that thing,' the poet said, 'I want you to write something in the voice of it. So if the bandstand could talk, what would it say, what would it see, what would it notice? How do you think the town hall feels when the sun starts to go down?' Because Brian felt sorry for him, and because there was something about the questions that intrigued him, he picked a black Bic out from the mug and started to write something. This seemed to spur on the other couple of men as well, and the other academics joined in too.

The poet didn't speak as they were writing; the only sound was the scratching of pens, the wheezing or coughing of one of the men, a cup being placed down a little too heavily on the table. They liked silences, Brian thought. They liked space. Conversation, talking, that was something that had to be worked through – they wrote down what he said, like a doctor listening to a patient; words were solid things, to be hacked at or pulled apart. But silence, the open space of it, they seemed to be willing to sit in it, to allow them to sit in it, and it never felt awkward, even when one of them ultimately cracked, and started talking. They wrote for about five minutes, Brian running out of things he could think to say after about two, doodling in the margins whilst the rest of them finished. He could feel the poet over his shoulder, looking down. When they got back together, the poet had looked at him and said, 'Brian, it looked like you were writing some really interesting things. Is there anything that you want to share?'

That silence again; they let it hang. Nobody else spoke. Brian cleared his throat.

'Well, I was thinking about the old away end at Oakwell,' Brian explained, 'before they built that new stand, and there was one match where we were getting thrashed by someone or other, and I kept looking out, over the heads of the away fans, because there was no roof at the time, and you could see these fields from the stand, and this old man was walking his dog, and he went past when it was 2–0 and then the next time he came past it was 6–0, and so I guess I was just thinking about what if the stand was describing that, I guess, what if the stand was bored of the match so it started looking the other way, and what sort of things might it see.'

'That sounds brilliant!' the poet replied, beaming. He looked over his shoulder to the other researchers for re-assurance, and they smiled and nodded too. 'I love that idea,' he went on, 'I think it asks such an interesting question, doesn't it, of history? The big event happening in one place, but what if we look somewhere else, what is it that we see then?'

'One man and his dog,' Brian replied, and smiled despite himself.

Fieldnotes: Coalfields

The current uses of the former coalfield sites in and around the town speak as metaphor to the psycho-geographical condition of the town as a whole. As one member of our team puts it as we drive back to Sheffield Station, the heavy irony of the word subsidence is that it is both a material condition of the land around these villages, but also a parable for a people unable to stop themselves from slipping into their own past.

Amitav Ghosh writes about the social imperatives for coal's success over the water-powered mills of the same age. He writes that 'coal-mills allowed mill owners to locate their factories in densely crowded cities, where cheap labor was easily available.' We argue that coal seams, rather than the mills they power, are partly accidents of geography, but what has replaced them in post-industrial landscapes, such as this town, is strikingly similar. The town was officially ranked as the lowest-paid place in the country in research conducted at the end of the last decade. We observe a cyclical effect of this: low wages in turn attract large multinational companies to base their call centres and distribution centres in 'brown belt' land which surrounds the constellation of villages on the outskirts of the town. They base themselves in these locations because they can pay less than in other places around the country, and thus wages are kept low. Ghosh quotes Malm, who wrote of 'the [steam] engine' as being 'a superior medium for extracting surplus wealth'. The choice of geographical location for industry now is less about extraction of surplus wealth than it is the deliberate blocking of its ability to accumulate. If you ever place a bet, or ring up your energy company, or order from certain online fast-fashion retailers, it is likely your life has crossed with that of someone from the town, even though it is not a place you imagine you would ever visit.

surveillance: gossip

When he got home to tell his wife about it, one of the regulars from the club said that it seemed like a really awkward meeting, I mean it's always awkward when they're together anyway, isn't it, Alex and Simon, he's so big and overweight and slouching and Simon so skinny and tall, it's like I've always said, isn't it, it's like they're not even related, like chalk and cheese, isn't it, if you didn't know, if you just passed them on the street. Anyway, it was just Simon and the other lad at first, I think I've seen him working security in the Alhambra, and they were sat close, not like on top of each other, but close like, and I made some joke saying I wonder if he's been caught shoplifting a dress or something, and they're in this really deep conversation anyway, both drinking these massive glasses of gin like it's water, Trip's stuck some fruit in it to try and make them look fancy, not like those you had in Leeds that time like, it'll only be the cheap stuff, you know how tight Trip is. Anyway, they're talking and stuff and at one point this other lad puts his hand on Simon's knee and then he looks up and I swear it's like he's seen a ghost, and then Simon whips around and it's his dad, it's Alex, and they both get proper flustered, and then Simon sort of half stands up behind the table, beckons him over, and we're over the other side so I can't really hear what's being said, but the Alhambra lad gets up and shakes Alex's hand and Alex sort of shuffles in between them so there's all three of them crammed in on one of them red leather sofas like, and every time Alex says something, the lad from the Alhambra, looks like he works out mind, well he laughs a little bit too loudly, or I'm guessing he does, the way he opens his mouth dead wide like, and Simon has this smile on his face like he's starting to relax a bit. There are a couple of times when Alex and the lad in the shirt are smiling at each other and Simon isn't smiling, has this look like he's been teased, and the two of them are smirking until Alex puts his arm around his lad or messes his hair, but this one time it's the lad in the shirt, the one from the Alhambra, who reaches over and squeezes Simon's knee and you can see Alex proper bristling at that, gets up and goes to the bar, pushing his way past them, and the two of them, Simon and the Alhambra lad, just looking at each other, and he mouths something like sorry at Simon, who just shrugs like it's no big deal, he's not going to say anything though, is he, he's always been soft like that. Alex gets a pint and they get some more gin, 'cos it's not like they've not had enough, and they're all talking away and at one point I just hear Alex shouting 'Police? The police?', and he gets up to go to the bar again, well I wasn't just sat staring like, but I heard the table shove back, those big black boots of his he insists on always wearing traipsing back over to Trip to get another round. He's well away by then, Alex is, and he's at the bar and he shouts over 'Here, Simon, maybe I should come and see your show tomorrow night,' and Simon looks dead awkward and just says 'I'm doing one here on Saturday, aren't I?', looking down at the floor, 'cos he is, isn't he, Trip's got him doing that one, I said didn't I, I got us tickets, anyway Alex shouts back over to him 'Yeah, but I can come and have a preview, can't I, as your dad, I get a special preview, right?'

He steps out into the long corridor of early dawn; wind galloping past him. Above, the sky is moving quickly and three doors down Pat is just closing his front door. Another few doors on there will be Harry and then Frank, and as they all turn the corner together Skip will be waiting, wanting to talk about last night's game. Some will mumble responses to him, most will stay quiet, incline their heads as someone else joins them and then keep on walking. More and more men fall out of their houses, pulling their jackets tight against the cold. Someone whistles; someone else coughs. Occasionally some stop, and lean for a moment on the low wall of a garden, the breeze all around them like hooves. Nobody waits for them, they just keep on walking. The village, on their shoulder now, still asleep, not watching the migration of tired bodies. One of the men once said he thought he could hear the coal cracking. Another man told him to stop talking daft. And beneath their feet, a mile down, money; to be counted at the surface, so they could be handed back the sleck.

Simon had no idea why his dad wanted to come to the show. He'd expected him to wake up the next morning, hungover and remorseful, and make up some sort of excuse like he always did to miss whatever the event of the day was. But he hadn't, and they'd got the train over together because his dad had insisted, even though Simon had said that he needed to be there really early to get sorted out and the club wouldn't even be open for a few hours and they probably wouldn't let him backstage, and Simon definitely didn't want him there while he was changing. Alex replied matter-of-factly that he didn't really want to be there for that either, no offence, and he'd just wander around for a bit, maybe go and sit in the Winter Garden if it was still open because he liked it in there and he could get a cup of tea, and Simon had sighed as they'd gone through the tunnel the train goes through just before it gets to Sheffield Station. They'd both sat quietly for the last few minutes of the journey into the city. Alex broke the silence as they were walking over the bridge towards the station entrance and said that he just wanted to see where his son worked, it was important to him, work was part of who Simon was and he wanted to know who his son was, and Simon said 'Well, you've never been to the call centre,' and Alex said 'Yeah, but this is different, isn't it?', and Simon asked why, and Alex said 'Well, because this is something you really care about.'

Simon couldn't disagree with that and he was still thinking about it as he left his dad at the Winter Garden and carried his bag up the steep hill towards the club. He'd never imagined his dad coming to see him. His mum maybe, even in the years when they'd never talked, or she'd text a couple of days after his birthday to say sorry she'd been so busy and she hoped he'd had a good day; sometimes he imagined glimpsing her at the bar, watching him on stage; sometimes he imagined her smiling. He'd be amazed if his dad even got in. He'd have to have a word with them on the door, make something up, say his dad was visiting from somewhere else, and so it was a special occasion and he wanted to come and see him perform. There was something in the embellishment that Simon thought might make things go a little more smoothly. He went through the process of getting ready backstage, suddenly aware that he was making himself up to be viewed. It seemed a ridiculous thing to realise, given the punters, but knowing his dad would be there, watching him, even though he wouldn't have a clue what was going on, Simon felt he had to be perfect. He paid extra attention to each detail, brushing the wig, lint-rolling the dress, and when it was his turn to go on stage and the music started playing, he stepped out.

The cage, always, is what he hates most. Waiting for faces to emerge, narrow-eyed against the light, crowding together in a space no bigger than the floor of his shed. Smelling the other men, their tiredness, and their yearning for the weekend, and their dreams, and their one-too-many beers for a weeknight, and their children, and last night's tea. Then the descent. He splashed his face before he left but it still felt as though the night had hung itself to dry around his shoulders. The earth rising up around him, through the bars, feeling like an animal and then coming to a stop as sudden as slamming into a wall. A man, like a shopkeeper in the morning, unlocking, letting them out. His pupils taking a while to adjust, waking up all over again. And then the walking. Headlamps pointing the way down the tunnels. No talking, a last intake of breath, grasping at what's left of the air from the surface. Readying. At least out of the cage he could move more freely, kick out the stiffness from his knees, wind his shoulder in a slow circle, preparing it for the swinging, the picking, the breaking. Sometimes the noise of the belts and the drills was so loud, it was like some beast come to life in the core of the earth, something massive, and hungry, clawing its way towards him.

Fieldnotes: Community

In the afternoon we decide to split up, half our team heading out to a small village museum, and the other half to Wentworth Castle, where there is a community art group we are keen to see.

Some of us head to the Maurice Dobson Museum. The eponymous Maurice Dobson was a former miner and Second World War veteran who, having been born in the next-door village, bought the grocery shop in 1956. He did so with his partner Fred Halliday, whom he had met whilst on active service. At a time when homosexuality was illegal, they set up shop together in the village and prided themselves on selling high-quality products to locals. Accounts differ on the impact of this within the community, some remembering an air of tolerance, some remembering Dobson wearing women's clothing as he walked about the streets, some remembering groups of young people gathering outside to torment Dobson and his partner. The shop is now a local museum, and when we visit one Saturday morning we are greeted by a husband-and-wife volunteer team; the grey-haired husband shows some of us around, whilst the wife, kind and softly spoken, makes toasted teacakes in the café for the rest of our party, and talks about the exhibition by a local artist displayed on the walls. The pictures are abstract; different shades demark different pieces of a view – a field, a road, the sky.

The museum houses a collection of antiques, collected by Dobson, alongside ephemera of local interest relating to the industry and personalities of the residents of the village over the past few centuries. School trips are the museum's most frequent and sizable audience, alongside older residents who remember Dobson and the grocery store he and Halliday ran. The museum strikes us as an important receptacle of lived history and local knowledge; if the national narrative of a place could be imagined as a long beach, then individual artefacts in museums such as this are the fragments of rock or mineral which the eye smooths out.

We think of creation myths, of the importance of a place telling the story of itself to future generations. We also consider the importance of who tells the story. History, of course, is not objective. A village does not have only one voice.

As if to prove this point, the other half of our group visit the Feels Like Home group, a support network for refugees and asylum seekers who are first settled in the town before deciding either to stay or to move on to other towns and cities where they have greater familial or national connections. The Feels Like Home group meets once a week, sometimes doing craft or writing activities, sometimes doing practical initiatives around public health or housing, sometimes simply just talking and catching up on the weeks that they have had. There are members from South America, Afghanistan, Syria, Iraq, Eastern Europe. Some for whom English was already one of their multiple languages when they arrived, some who are learning more week by week.

We join in on a session where the group are working on a craft project for a forthcoming exhibition at a local public garden; they are using their memories of their homeland and their home nation's national flower to design a flag which celebrates it. Children and babies are welcome at the group; the older ones play together but the younger ones stay with their parents as they talk and create on the long fold-out plastic tables which sit in the middle of the room. Sometimes, when someone needs to leave to use the bathroom, or goes into the small kitchenette just off to the side to make more tea, a baby is passed to someone else, or we witness different adults taking turns in leading games or walks with the older children.

We note that one of the narratives which often emerges in post-industrial spaces, such as this town, is that community no longer exists in the way that it did, that the decline of heavy industry directly precipitated the decline of community. We propose that this is not the case, that we perhaps just require a recalibration of what we believe the community to look like or be.

In between numbers, or when a newer queen was having a go at holding the drunk room's attention, Simon would stand backstage and just look in the mirror. In those moments, in full drag, he was himself and not himself. He still had his eyes, just larger in the make-up, rounder. He still had his face, just more angular, contoured so it seemed sharper. In some lights, in some wigs, he was his auntie or his grandma. Not himself because he was Puttana, and she was brasher, broader, louder than Simon, and yet he was more himself too, because weren't these the things that he'd tried for so long to hide.

In school he'd had this thing inside him that he was so scared of other people finding out, so each day had felt like an endurance test in holding his breath, in not being seen, in being quiet and meek and hoping to simply not be noticed. That loudness, that comedy, that fearlessness was in there, and in the club, in this wig, in these heels, he didn't have to hide it, he could bring it up from deep down inside him, let it fire him up, let it consume him. It wasn't 'costume', he often thought, because costume was something more like a disguise, to hide yourself, whereas now, in the mirror, he felt so much more himself than he ever did. This was it, this was him.

Simon knew there was a different world of drag he wanted to explore, away from the TV shows of it, away from performing to hen parties and groups of drunk lads. He knew it could be political, more edgy, that there was a way in which it could bring to the surface things that might otherwise be hidden. What was it his English teacher had said once? The fool in Shakespeare always carries the truth. They nearly always had a Yorkshire accent too, Simon remembered, because apparently people found that funnier.

Great drag, he knew, was art, but art cost money. So until then there were the OnlyFans videos, the taking of the calls of the people betting more money on a single horse race than Simon had ever seen, and there were nights like this, the small changing room, this mirror, that stage. There was the applause, sometimes cheering. More often the drunken background chatter that wasn't paying any attention to him at all. There was the taking of a deep breath, the stepping out onto the raised wooden platform, there was the light coming over him like a wave, until it was all he could see.

Tonight, he deliberately went further forward than he usually would have done, so the lights were on the top of his head rather than directly in his eyes. He didn't see his dad at first and assumed he'd chickened out, or got drinking somewhere, or was standing outside smoking and debating whether he really had the guts to come in. Simon started lip-synching while scanning the room and then he saw him, right at the back, sitting on a bar stool, a pint in his hand, and he was looking over, too far back to make out any expression on his face, but he was there, watching, in a shirt he thought was smart but still those fucking boots he insisted on wearing everywhere, whatever the occasion, and Simon froze for a moment but only for a moment and then went back into the song, feeling each word, drawing the lyrics out in the air with his arms, stepping through the grey wool of the smoke machine on the floor. Mostly people talked amongst themselves, half watching, but some sang along, imitating the moves, the old regulars and the first-timers watching it all, giving it their whole attention. And Dad, Simon thought, as he finished with a flourish and the DJ started playing something that would get everyone up and dancing again.

He texted his dad and told him to wait outside while he sorted himself out and they could head off together. He'd asked the manager if it was OK if he didn't stay the rest of the night, he just wanted to get home. His dad replied that he was OK at the bar, he still had his pint to finish, and the dregs were still lingering in the glass when Simon came out into the club from backstage. There was a man standing next to him, leaning over slightly as Alex was saying something, as though he was struggling to hear over the noise of the club. Simon was disorientated, not used to being there when people were dancing; his nights there were backstage, onstage, leaving through the rear exit. Alex saw Simon coming over and turned away from the man, downed his pint and stood up. Simon walked over to his dad, taking a deep breath and asking him, as casually as he could, like he might about a football game, 'Well, how was that then? Looks like you made a friend.' Simon's face was still bright red from taking off the make-up, so his embarrassment didn't show through like it might have. 'He was just asking me what time it was, reckoned he was meeting someone here – think he's probably been stood up, poor lad.' Simon looked momentarily at the man at the bar, and then back to his dad. 'Come on then, what did you think?' 'I thought it was brave,' Alex said, and smiled, as though the word didn't need any further explanation.

They left together, talking easily about the evening, Alex suggesting they head to the club once they got back to Barnsley, and Simon feeling so at ease with his dad, not wanting it to end, agreeing, saying yes, of course, and sure, yes, he'd invite Ryan. His dad asked Simon about his drag name, and he had to try and explain the pun to him and then when his dad asked where it had come from, Simon had to tell him about a play they'd done at college, and how Puttana was this funny, sexy character in it, so he'd just decided to go with that. Alex told his son that he didn't think that made much sense, though, it didn't really say anything about who he was, and Simon said well maybe that's the point, being someone else. And they'd sat for a while before Alex had spoken up again, saying that shouldn't his drag name be something more local, didn't he want to be proud of where he was from. And Simon had asked him what sort of name and his dad had replied well, you know, a proper Barnsley drag name, and Simon had said what like Cheryl Coal, and Alex suggested Slag Heap, which made them both howl with laughter, and then Simon suggested Martha Scargill and they both just sat there for a moment, before bursting out laughing again.

Simon had expected a lecture, about how this wasn't really a career, and had he thought any more about going for the supervisor position at work, and you know it was not that anyone minded, but it was all so big, so loud, so *open*. He'd worried that his dad would get so nervous and feel so out of place that he'd drink too much and start going on about his mum, those half phrases he'd mumble sometimes when he'd been drinking, 'if she hadn't have left', or 'if we'd stayed together', 'if I hadn't . . .'

But there was none of that, just a kind of lightness Simon hadn't sensed in him for years, making the jokes he always used to about the posh voice the automatic announcement used to pronounce Wombwell and Elsecar as it rattled off the list of coming destinations. At Chapeltown a group of young lads got on; they kept looking over at them both every time they laughed. Simon noticed one of them catch his dad's eye, and after that his dad had seemed quieter; still himself, but smaller maybe.

surveillance: CCTV

The three of them, Alex, Simon and Ryan, hadn't been sober enough to give Trip a proper account of what happened, though he could piece things together from the fragments of story they each stumbled back into the club with. A few years back there'd been some trouble with anti-social behaviour outside, kids kicking the bins over, setting small fires in the smoking area, and so he'd invested in his own cameras. It wasn't proper CCTV, that would have been too expensive, but small, unobtrusive cameras that kept their gaze on specific parts of the interior and exterior of the club. He'd put one of them just above the side entrance to look out onto the pavement, where the bus stop was. Some of the older punters didn't like standing there alone after closing time, especially in winter when it was dark, so it was more to reassure them than anything else. That evening, after everyone had gone and the air settled back down from the excitement that had pulsed through it, he scrolled back through the camera feed.

Alex is leaning up against the bus stop pole, Ryan and Simon holding hands. The harsh shine of a streetlight and the low-quality footage makes it seem as though the figures are glowing somehow, illuminated, almost angelic. The camera shows three heads all turning at once towards the road, as though a sudden noise has startled them, then their heads return quickly to each other but then Simon turns back again. He takes a step into the estuary of the bus lay-by; Ryan holds him back. There are some arms being waved, a 'wanker' sign from Alex, Ryan pointing and shaking his head, Simon stood half on and half off the kerb.

They stay that way for a few moments, whatever it is off camera provoking them seeming to pass, but then Alex steps across the road; the narrow gaze of the camera means he's just out of shot, but after thirty seconds he stumbles back into the frame, as though pushed. He steps forward again, is pushed back. He is standing taller now, not slouching, and despite the pixelated image you can see him puffing out his chest a bit, trying to broaden his shoulders, take up more space.

Then Trip watches as two men stumble back, Alex and another man. At first it could seem as though they are embracing, rocking slowly back and forth, but then Ryan tries to come between the men and Simon pulls him back. He and Ryan both have their hands out, an offering of peace, pushing their palms down in a gesture that is calling for calm. There's a lull, it seems as though it's worked, but then the video shows Alex push the other man hard, so he's out of the frame again.

Alex stands back, turns around to Ryan and Simon, puts a hand on both their shoulders. The other man comes back into the frame, a hand raised, and Alex is jolted forward into the bus stop pole he'd been leaning against and Simon and Ryan push the stranger away. They try to hold on to Alex as he turns and walks towards the figure, who's on his back now, on the floor, legs in shot but his torso and head out of frame. Trip watches as Alex gets on his knees, over the man, straddling him, pulling back his arm and releasing it, over and over again, a fist landing somewhere just out of the picture, over and over again, a fist swung high and dropped like a pickaxe. Then Ryan and Simon pulling him up, Ryan turning around to shout something, bundling Alex back through the door into the club.

Trip held his cursor over the file, dragged it to the wastebin. Asked the computer to permanently erase it.

surveillance: gossip

Well, who knows what really went on, one of the regulars
was saying to his mum after checking that her evening
carer had definitely been to call this time, and was she
really sure, well I mean he was drunk when he left, well
in fact truth be told he was drunk when he got here, Alex
I mean, 'cos he'd been gone watching Simon over in
Sheffield, you know those performances he does, and that
lad from the Alhambra was sat here drinking, waiting for
'em, was almost last orders by the time they got here, but
they managed to squeeze in a couple, and we were just
finishing up like, and then there's all this commotion, and
shouting, didn't know what was going on, and Alex comes
back in, with Simon and that other lad, one of his arms
over each of their shoulders, and the blood gushing down.
And of course Trip's straight over to him, holding that bar
rag up to his face to stop the bleeding and I remember
thinking to myself that God I bet that stinks, and all four
of them go and sit in that far booth, and Alex is sat with

his head tilted back and all four of them are talking at once so you can't really hear anything proper what's going on, it's just like this fog of words that's drifting over, but Trip told me later it was some spicehead walking up from the Rec and he's seen Simon and Ryan holding hands as they were waiting for the bus and apparently Alex had told them that maybe they wanted to be a bit careful like, why attract attention like that, but Trip said Simon had just looked at his dad like he was from another century or something and Trip didn't say anything because you know what he's like with confrontation, and anyway Trip then says that Ryan kept pushing about calling the police, it was common assault he reckoned, and Alex said he'd just slipped into the bus stop pole and Simon said no dad you were pushed and Ryan said yeah it's common assault, and probably breach of the peace for what he was shouting at me and Si too, and Alex said well what about what I did to him, and they all said self-defence, and Trip said there was an odd look on Alex's face as though it took him a moment to work out who 'Si' was because he wasn't used to him being called that and Alex just kept insisting, in this odd, nasal tone because he was pinching his nose to try and stop the blood, that he's not having the pigs come down here and what would they do anyway and Trip reckons Ryan just can't get that into his head, says he just keeps saying but Mr Banks, using his proper name like 'cos he's still trying to impress him isn't he, 'cos he's with Simon now isn't he, he keeps saying Mr Banks you were attacked, and that man was clearly on drugs and we should call the police, and Simon isn't really saying anything at this point, just holding that stinking flannel to his dad's face, and eventually Trip says that Alex suggests they just call Brian, and get him to come down and take his brother home, and Ryan just can't get his head around it, and Alex says that last time he was close enough to the police for them to do anything he ended up with much worse than a bit of a bloody nose, and well Trip says that shut Ryan up for a bit.

That night, when Alex gets home, and he's sitting on his settee, this is what he remembers. Simon's hand in Ryan's. A shout from over the road. More noise. The man's arms coming towards him, the bus stop pole, the back of his own head hitting the metal. Something tearing open. He feels hands, he doesn't know whose, on his collar, on his back, pulling him away. He sees Trip's mucky flannel coming towards him as though someone might be trying to suffocate him. He sees the muddy stain of beer, the lights of the club through the fraying patches of cloth. In some moments that raised hand is a stick, sometimes a baton, sometimes the sound of his head against the metal is the sound of a shield being struck. Sometimes the engine of a passing car is a shout. There are some moments the wind sounds as though it's all around him, each gust striking his face, before moving quickly past him.

He steps out into the long corridor of early dawn; the street stretching downwards, pointing him to where he's headed. Above, the sky is the embers of a furnace and three doors down Pat is just closing his front door. Another few doors on there will be Harry, no Frank today since he hurt his leg, and so there'll be one fewer as they turn the corner, Skip already ahead of them and all of them too tired to think about running to catch up with him. Nobody speaks; they incline their heads as someone else joins them and then keep on walking. More and more men fall out of their houses, faces tired but clean, for now. Someone whistles, someone else coughs. Occasionally some stop, and lean for a moment on the low wall of a garden, pretending they need to double-check their snap tin or enjoy a long drag on their roll-up, the smoke coming in hacking bursts into the air. Nobody waits for them. The village, on their shoulder now, still sleeping, not watching this procession of the knackered, their inevitable destination. One of the men once said he thought he could hear the coal whispering. Another man told him to stop talking daft.

126

And beneath their feet, a mile down, other men, their breath the breath of the soil, their sweat dripping like time from their brows.

Simon had read some comments online about people who'd done what the internet had dubbed 'Thatcher Drag'; a lot of the criticism seemed to be that even in drag she was still being celebrated, or maybe even softened, made a figure of fun in a way that somehow took away from what she'd done to towns like his. He sat in the living room of his flat, Ryan not long having left to go to work, cup of coffee still cooling on the kitchen table, the sort you were probably meant to put on a balcony, except this flat didn't have one, just bars across the window so from a distance, with no sense of perspective, you could be fooled into thinking there might be one.

Simon was brushing the wig, the long backwards wave of it, making sure there were no strays, no kinks. Thatcher's hair on a Styrofoam mannequin on his knee, some daytime quiz show on the TV. Someone was in with a chance of winning £2,000, and they were saying they'd use it to take their mum away because they'd never had the chance to go away when they were young. Well, I wish you all the luck in the world the host was saying, that sounds like a really lovely thing to do, isn't he lovely everyone? Right, your categories are cars, flowers, oceans or footballers, which one would you like to choose?

Simon had messaged his dad first thing. His Uncle Brian had been drinking, and so hadn't been able to come, so he and Ryan had got his dad home in a taxi and asked if he needed anything but he said no he was fine, it was just a bump, just a bit of a nosebleed, they shouldn't worry, and they'd both known to stop going on and they'd let him be. He'd replied this morning to say he was fine, and asked how him and Ryan were too. That sort of stuff shouldn't happen, his dad had said, I know you were just holding hands, but you should be careful. Maybe, his dad had said, he could even think about asking Trip to postpone the show. What if someone got really aggy, and it kicked off?

Each revolution of Simon's arm, each stroke, cemented the hair more firmly in place, all of it swept away from her face, like a helmet, those two iconic pearl earrings like shields. And as he brushed he thought that it wasn't neces-sarily always right, that doing Thatcher didn't have to be a celebration. A stray hair rose up into the light, wafted like a thin scarf in a breeze, until he pinched its fibres between his fingers, and smoothed it back into the rest.

He remembered when she'd died, how people had been

out in the streets, that there'd been an effigy of her burned. His performance wouldn't be an effigy, but maybe a gay man in drag repeating the words of the Section 28 speech showed up that she'd been performing something too, that she recognised gender as something malleable, had vocal lessons to lower her voice, watched her posture. Because maybe, Simon thought, as the contestant on the screen who wanted to take his mum on holiday was wrongly identifying Beckham and not Ronaldo as the highest-paid footballer of all time, and the host had this look in his eyes like he wanted him to realise it was the wrong answer but he wasn't allowed to say anything so he just kept repeating is that the answer you want to lock in, are you sure? Because there was nothing else he could do except let it play out, the audience groaning, the contestant leaving with a trophy and no money, because maybe, Simon thought, if something was interrupted, if someone had different words to speak, maybe the wheel would begin to slowly turn the other way, if only for one night.

Brian had thought about not going back for the third and final session, but he always liked to see something through. Today the team had said they didn't have anything special planned, but they felt it would be great to come together in order to 'tie up the loose ends' and perhaps 'plot some ways forward'. Two of the other blokes had come back, and the woman from the food bank as well. They each had a clipboard, and on it a piece of paper similar to one they'd been given in the first session but with subtly different questions. 'What do you feel you have learned?' instead of 'What are you hoping to learn?' 'Have your memories of the town, the strike or the pits changed because of the work we've done together?' instead of 'What are your memories of the town, the strikes, or the pits?' There was a blank space at the bottom, where they had to write a memorable phrase or something somebody had said, something that had stuck with them.

Brian looked around at the other two, dutifully filling in their clipboards, the academics standing around the tea urn, trying not to look as though they were looking, checking in on how they were getting on. Brian found he wanted to fill it in sincerely, wanted to remember one of the phrases from the poems, or the old names of the shops. He began to write down a few of the words of dialect they'd gathered in one exercise, words he hadn't thought about for years, since his parents were alive. Words that felt to him like coins; like that Roman horde they'd dug up in the village just down the road, parts of history, buried just below the surface, recognisable but different. Words like chelp and morngy and laik. Brian loved to remember them because he could picture the exact shape of his dad's mouth as he said them, the exact angle of his mum's head as she received them. They were physical words, they were words that were built of the body, and of the ground, words that had been lived before they'd been spoken.

There was something else he wanted to write, though; the gap they'd left on the page was quite big and he had this overwhelming urge to fill it. There was something in the poetry exercises they'd done, where they'd used the cards as well. The poet who came in got them writing lines about things as they used to be, how they were now, what they might be like in the future, and in a moment of vagueness he'd said 'now try and bring all those together'. Brian hadn't known what to do at first, hadn't really known what that meant, kept thinking of words that might rhyme, but then there'd been this moment, a sudden arrival into

his mind from who knew where, and he wrote down then
what he wrote down here again.

Pits close: we still sink into them

Subscribers to Simon's OnlyFans got a message trailing an 'exciting new video' that he'd be releasing at 8 p.m. If anyone went to his Twitter and retweeted the still image of his and Ryan's bodies to their followers they'd be entered into a draw to win a month's free subscription, and a 'special thankyou' emailed directly to them. That 'special thankyou' was something Simon had already recorded earlier, the phone placed down on the floor, looking up at him, the front camera on so he could look down at himself as he recorded. White, shin-high socks, like a footballer's, and a pair of white y-fronts were all he was wearing. He leant down slowly towards the camera, and anyone watching with any interest would have seen the way his stomach tensed as he moved, as he desperately tried to keep its definition as he folded towards his audience. Simon winked and mouthed the words 'thank you', before moving his foot closer and closer towards the camera, then he kicked it over and the screen went dead.

He'd had to send the video to about twelve different people who'd done as he asked on Twitter, and got a couple of new sign-ups; he was edging perilously close to triple figures now and sometimes wondered about being recognised by someone. Now, at 8 p.m., Simon clicked the button that released the video to the subscribers, and he imagined it like a coin in one of the penny-slot arcade machines, tumbling through the invisible wires of the internet, landing on people's phones, or laptops or tablets. The show at the club was so close, he was glad of the momentary distraction.

Anyone eager enough to open the video straight away was greeted by an image of a mirrored wardrobe. Two doors of glass, in which a camera on a tripod was reflected back, filming itself. Simon walks into shot, approaching the wardrobe, so that in the reflection he is topless and moving towards himself, and in the lens of the camera, through which the subscribers are watching, he is moving away. Another figure can be seen lurking in the corner of the image, in shadow, until he begins to move further in, approaching at an angle so that the view the camera has is only of Simon; only the mirror holds the two figures. Simon and Ryan. Or to the subscribers, Simon and a stranger. Ryan, in a pair of black boxer shorts, held tight across his thighs, topless, the fuzz of body hair seen as a faint blur through the lens, has a balaclava pulled over his head. The balaclava means no kissing, almost no sound at all, as Simon turns side-on to the camera, his face as though on a coin, in profile, and Ryan's boxers are slowly pulled down to lay around his ankles, and he springs semi-hard into Simon's waiting hand. Simon makes eye contact as he lets Ryan's dick seem as though it's forcing his lips apart. Ryan's hand rests on the top of Simon's head and he raises his other hand, brings a phone up, and starts recording a top-down view from his chest. The subscribers get this altered view, the camera close enough to pick up little bits of black fluff stuck to Ryan's hand as it turns and tousles Simon's hair; remnants of the balaclava hastily pulled on before the filming started.

If the subscribers stayed right to the end of the film they'd get to see both of them facing away from the tripod, one face and one hidden face in the mirror, and then the very end, after the climax, back to the camera phone, pointing down as they kiss, towards their feet, where the balaclava sat wrinkled on the floor.

In the unedited version that Simon always kept on his phone, there was the moment Simon grabs the phone from Ryan, turns it around on him, and Ryan is smiling, almost laughing, bits of wool from the balaclava stuck to his sweating face, like the first stubble of an adolescent. Simon zooms in on him until the picture is just a blur, until it's too close to see anything at all, and then he presses stop.

Brian was half listening to the group conversation, half lost in his own thoughts, and the words came to him intermittently, as though through static. He heard key phrases: 'we've tried to come at this idea in different ways', 'we wanted to know what the legacy was, what the true impact was', 'sometimes the truth is different to different people', 'you were really there, this isn't a newspaper report'.

Brian sighed, probably louder than he'd intended to, and everyone turned to look at him. He said he was sorry, went back to looking at his feet. The academics went back to talking amongst themselves, or to the group, but really amongst themselves, Brian thought. The next phrase that dropped made him look up: 'when we were there, doing this similar work, but over there, and it's true that there were some bad memories too, but one participant . . .', they always said participant when they meant person, '. . .

well, they said that the strike had been the best time of their life'.

There was a little bit of murmuring at that, and Brian didn't really know what to say, but then a word came to him. 'Community,' he said, before he'd really processed it. Everyone looked to him. 'Community is probably what they were talking about right, the soup kitchens, the solidarity, the sense of one collective fight. You know there were a couple of times we were even on the news, I saw myself, well the back of my head like, and I remember mum calling me in to look and she says "Is that you?" and I said "I think so." The BBC news. When would that ever happen normally?' Nobody else spoke, that silence again, but this time it felt to Brian like he had a way through it. 'Just felt like we were all in it together, you know.' The younger of the academics looked up from his notepad. 'That's a phrase that's been about in the last few years, isn't it, we're all in this together.' 'Yeah,' Brian replied, feeling his voice grow inside him now, 'but when they say it, they mean themselves, don't they, they're all in it together, against us, against people like us, but here, back then, we really were all in it together, weren't we?'

Another man, sat on his own fading plastic chair, said quietly: 'Aye, if you knew the right people. Don't remember ever getting a food parcel or any handout from the union up our end.'

The younger academic, perhaps sensing a brewing tension and wanting to extinguish it before it could light up, jumped in: 'This is the root of what we're interested in, I think: personal narratives of a time when so often there's a dominant narrative that gets told, so all these little bits, these other truths, these flints of personal experience, they get lost, get crushed under the weight of the overarching narrative.' Brian sighed again, and this time when everyone looked over to him he didn't look down at the ground, he didn't say sorry.

'You keep using this word narrative,' he said, not looking at any of them in particular. 'You keep saying truth, you keep asking us the same things in different ways. What is it that you want from us?' Brian's voice rose louder than he'd intended it to. 'What story is it that you want from us?' His chair squeaked against the floor, as though for emphasis.

The way the group looked to Brian reminded him of the way Simon had looked at him when he was a child, wanting his uncle to tell him what came next.

He stoops to gather something up at his feet when it happens, so there's a split second when he's still awake and everyone else is already buried. It comes at them like a wave, like they're already underneath a wave and the wave has decided to break and break over them. The steel and the wood first, crashing down like ships, and then the rocks and rubble and the whole earth, down on them, like flicking off a light, and because he's stooping there's a split second where he sees Pat fold like an accordion, sees the new lad hit the deck, arms over his head and even though he knows it won't make a difference he does the same, throws himself onto the floor, and it isn't the impact of a beam, or the fear, it's the weight of the world on his back, as piss runs down his leg, blood from his temple, it's the muck that compacts itself inside his lungs, like a gardener patting down the earth around something newly planted. It's all that weight, of time, of history, pushing down on his back. On his spine. Forcing the life out.

Brian had let that silence sit for what felt to him like years, though it must only have been two or three minutes. The other blokes looked down at the floor, and the ones from the university weren't staring at him, that would have been too intimidating, but into the silence, as though they knew something was going to emerge from it and they just had to be patient. Brian inhaled deeply; there was a sound from inside like someone scrunching an old paper bag. 'You already know the story anyway, all these guys do.' Brian waited for one of them to respond, for someone to stop him, but nobody did. He inhaled again, the paper bag scrunching in his chest. 'There was an explosion, they reckon it was one of the fans, that it must not have been working right or something, and there was this build-up of methane and then it just blew, roof came in while they were working on the face. Crushed them. I think there's a couple they never even managed to find. They're still down there.'

Silence again, nobody trying to fill it. Brian was studying his shoes. It was the younger academic who spoke up. 'It's so interesting, isn't it, how some things are remembered by a town and some things just get forgotten.' 'Who's forgotten?' Brian snapped back. 'Well, maybe not forgotten exactly, but sometimes disasters, Aberfan is a good example perhaps, get baked into the collective memory of a place, but this disaster, I knew about it from some of the reading I've done but it doesn't seem to be something that is at the forefront of people's minds.' More silence, Brian studying more of his shoes. When he spoke again, his voice was quieter, hoarse. 'Aberfan was kids, they were all just kids . . .' Brian sat back in his chair. 'People do know, they just don't want to remember, there's a difference.' The older of the academics began to speak then, but Brian cut him off. 'No, just look, what's the point? What is it that you're asking of us here? You want to know why people don't go around talking about the explosion? Because why would they, because they have to get on with their lives, don't they, they don't want to be thinking about the fact they're literally walking over the tops of bodies that were crushed to death beneath them. How could you go and get a few bits from the shop if that was in your head every single day? People have to get on, people have to live, there's no point digging all this up, is there?'

The older academic had his hands out, palms raised, was talking in a slow and quiet voice. 'You're absolutely right, that anger, that hurt, you're absolutely right, and I hear you. Our idea was that if we found new ways of thinking about the past, if we could do it through poetry, or by reframing memory, if we could find a new language for how we articulate these memories, then it might give us new ways of moving forward, ways of imagining different futures.' Brian looked at him, considered this for a moment. 'I don't want new ways to talk about what happened, I don't want to talk about it. We were just kids anyway, we barely remember it.' 'Who were?' the younger academic asked. 'Me and Alex, just kids when it all happened. So you're asking what I remember of it? It was the seventies, I was a teenager.'

'And despite that,' the younger academic said, 'despite knowing about that disaster, you still went and worked there. There's a poet I really like called Thom Gunn, and he wrote a lot about death, and there's this line of his: "I am confused to be attracted by my own annihilation . . .".' He looked around, conscious he was losing the room, catching the eye of the older academic, who just shrugged, so he went on 'It just struck me as something similar, being drawn towards something that might kill you.' 'What else was there?' Brian asked him. 'You're talking as though there were all these choices laid out before us, university, moving away . . . I just remember waiting for Mum to get the bus back from the club, this club, where you're sat now, where the police and the bosses were liaising about who was still down there, who'd they'd found. I remember wanting to go but Mum saying I had to stay with Alex, make sure he was all right. It must have been turned midnight by the time she got back and we were both in bed and I just didn't want her to tell us anything so I whispered to Alex that we should both pretend to be asleep, we shared the back bedroom, and she came in, went straight to bed, and laying there that night I kept imagining what it might be like to be in a coffin, to be in a tomb, to be trapped under tons and tons of rubble, unable to move, to be dug up in thousands of years like those mummies in Egypt that we were learning about in school. To be history. It makes my chest tight to think of it, but I get scared of forgetting it and it creeps back in until I feel like I can't breathe. I know it's not healthy, that I'm trapped in it, but what can I do? There's always this weight. I know Alex feels it too. He always said that's why he wanted to work there, Alex always wanted that specific pit, he said it made him feel closer to him somehow, made him feel as though he wasn't really gone. He's always been soft like that. You just have to get on . . . you just have to get on, don't you, go to the football, go to work, get the few bits from the shops. Bury your dead. Move on.'

The other participants were looking at him now. 'Your dad was . . .' the older academic began, then stopped himself. 'What was his name?' he asked. 'Brian,' Brian replied.

Out of boredom more than necessity really, Ryan was completing his routine of getting rid of the lingering men from the toilets. He'd done his waiting outside, had wandered in and done his sweep of the premises, and was now waiting again on the far wall, one shoe to the white tile, thumbing through his phone, looking artificially distracted as he kept an eye on who was coming and going.

One man ran in, carrying a small child in front of him like a bomb, and a couple of minutes later a woman came up to stand near Ryan and the man re-emerged, carrying the child in a calmer manner, placing him into the buggy before they left. Ryan waited a couple more minutes until another man, perhaps in his thirties, came out wiping his hands on his trousers, keeping his head down as he hurried to the exit. An older man next, maybe sixty, in an ill-fitting suit, carrying a briefcase that looked leather but was probably faux; old-fashioned enough to still have those dials on the top that you could turn to lock it. Ryan waited another thirty seconds or so and then, satisfied that was the last of them, he began to walk over to the toilets, to do a final check. Just when he was almost at the door, a rushing figure walked directly into him.

Ryan staggered back and for a brief second the rushing man looked at him, flushed, before half jogging, half walking out of the entrance, heavy black boots echoing off the polished floors. Ryan turned to see him leave and then walked slowly away, a faint wet handprint drying on his jacket from where the man had steadied himself. Even in the rush of the coming together and departing of the bodies, Ryan knew it had been Alex. Alex's hand on his chest. Alex looking into Ryan's eyes. A look of fear, as though Ryan was a wall coming unstoppably towards him.

Call it what you will. An explosion. An earth slip. A roof collapse. An accident. An incident. A disaster. A tragedy. Say investigators, say rescuers, say widows. Say family, say street, say community.

Simon Smith, 42

Norman Drury, 55

Pat Williamson, 19

Kenneth 'Skip' Baker, 45

Brian Banks, 51

There are mornings nobody steps out.

When the dawn is an empty corridor.

Everyone's door staying closed.

The next day, when Alex is at home, sitting on his settee, this is what he remembers. At first nothing, the long tunnel of darkness surrounding him. Then the same darkness but with chinks of light, as though he was a boy and back in his dad's pigeon shed. Then it's Brian's arm over his shoulder, then the wank mag they'd snuck in from school. He's still feeling his breath come back down to normal, eyes closed, and soon it's the smell that envelops him, the chlorine-clean smell of the toilets, and what it masks. He sees himself, outside of himself, walking down between the row of urinals and the row of cubicles, nervous like he's walking down the tunnel at Oakwell for the first game of the season. In the panic of leaving he can't remember which cubicle it was he chose, the second-to-end one or the end one, but in the memory he opts for the end one, goes in and locks the door.

Behind his closed eyes, the graffiti and carvings on the back of the door and lined-plywood walls float up like smoke. A profanity, a phone number, the crudely drawn logo of a visiting football team. All he can hear is his breath, and he's not sure if it's his breath in real life as he's sitting on the settee or his breath as he's waiting on the closed lid of the toilet seat, trousers around his ankles to make things seem more natural. Sometimes, sitting like that, something biological kicks in, and he gets the urge to actually go, and so he flushes and goes back out and washes his hands and then back into the cubicle again. But this time he's just sitting, his breath or not really his breath coming in shallow draughts in and out. Then it's the hand that intrudes into his vision. Coming through the low slot between the partition and the floor. Severed of anything now, like a nightmarish puppet, and then he can see himself move his foot towards the open palm, slower, the way it sometimes is in dreams when it seems like you're wading through fog. The tap of the foot against the open palm, once, twice, to signal yes, and then he sees himself fall to his knees, facing the body on the other side of the wall. Slipping himself out of his jeans, trying to angle himself without straining his back so the hand can reach up and cup him, then take him into his hand, rough but not unpleasantly so, and start slowly stroking. The breathing again, heavier now, either his then or his now, and then the deliberate cough of warning, loud shoes on the tiles. How, when he'd burst through the doors of the shopping centre onto the street, not looking back to see if Ryan's gaze was following him, the daylight had felt too bright, too warm, as though he were naked, entirely exposed.

And the nights of coming in late, after being at a bar, trying to sneak up the stairs, trying not to wake Simon, or Simon's mum, and more often than not just falling asleep on the settee, being woken up in the morning by slamming doors, by Simon whispering 'but why would he sleep down there', smelling himself, wanting to throw up. He sees, and thinks he will see every night for the rest of his life, her face, the night he told her, no, the night she found him out, after years of knowing really and not saying, and said she couldn't stay, said she didn't know what he'd tell Simon, 'Just say I've got a job or I've run off with someone, don't tell him *this*, he won't understand, I just, I can't stay here.' The night she'd said 'look after him', as though she was placing a young bird in his hands.

He sees the night, maybe a year after that, in the Chicago Rock Café, one Tuesday when it was gay night, after a match at Oakwell, and him and Brian and some of the lads went there because it was the only place left open. Being too rowdy; staring, pointing, laughing and then, at one point, when Alex was in the toilet, partly out of embarrassment as well as need, them getting kicked out, too far gone to notice if anyone was missing. Alex staying, sitting at the bar nursing a pint and he still sees it so clearly now, the older man, maybe fifty, sitting beside him, sipping his drink silently, and then a hand on his knee, and Alex flinching at first but then moving his leg back, so the man could just rest it there. He still sees the relief in the man's eyes, then the fear as Alex stands up, towers over him, and then the smile when Alex says 'shall we go then, do you

151

live round here'. When he closes his eyes, Alex can still picture the pale length of the man's back beneath him, the faded tattoo of a compass on his shoulder, the way he trembled, as though the flat was too cold, how he didn't ask his name.

Simon had read once how anxiety and excitement are really just separated by the thinnest seam of feeling, how it's hard to distinguish between the two. His turn as Maggie was here, Simon as Puttana Short Dress, as Margaret Thatcher. Performing elsewhere, in the dark, in a different city, felt safer somehow, less exposing. Here it would be people he knew, the club regulars, Uncle Brian, his dad had said he would go, Ryan, and maybe even a couple of the women from the call centre who'd shown a brief interest when he'd mentioned it. There was still a small part of him that hoped his mum might show up, even after twenty years, but he knew she wouldn't. And if she did that meant his dad definitely wouldn't come. Two decades on, whatever she'd done, he still couldn't face her.

He'd rather a room of strangers. It was always harder to be watched by people you knew, Simon thought, because they'd see straight through any act, anything that felt inauthentic.

When Trip had first asked him, months ago, if he fancied doing something at the bar, it had seemed impossibly far away. Trip was trying to get more money in but also, he said, a younger crowd and a couple of the bars in town had drag acts on, and not just on gay night either, and it seemed to be going OK for them and there hadn't been any trouble and so did he fancy giving it a go. Simon had been a few gins deep with his dad by that point so he'd just agreed, and Trip had known to leave before Alex had the chance to raise any objections. Then the weeks had ticked by in rehearsals, and he'd known he wanted to do something a bit different, something that maybe showed people that drag might have something to say, that he could do more than just entertain the drunks in the dark in a city where he didn't even live.

And now it was today, and Ryan was coming, which was an extra layer of nerves, and they'd never really solved the argument last Sunday in Sheffield, he'd just ended up sort of accepting it, agreeing to not agree.

Ryan had said he'd bring the camera and the tripod and film the show. Simon thought if he could edit it into something professional and get it up on YouTube, get it shared around socials, then maybe he could book a gig in London, maybe even get on TV. When he'd said this to Ryan, Ryan had asked him why he would want to release something online that he didn't really do and Simon had asked him what he meant and Ryan had said that the stuff he'd seen him do in Sheffield last week, like that was his show, that was how he made money, and this wasn't really what he did, was it, it was a kind of a one-off thing, and Simon had said but that stuff isn't the stuff I want to really be doing and this stuff is, and Ryan had just kind of made a face and Simon had asked him what and Ryan had said it was nothing, but maybe it was just a little bit cliched, wasn't it, a lad from Barnsley, doing Thatcher, the miners, it's what they'd expect someone like you to do, isn't it? And Simon hadn't really known what to say to that, but he said he thought it maybe wasn't obvious or why weren't any of the other queens who worked in town doing it? And anyway, at least it meant that he might get on TV, might have a chance of being seen. Or maybe it would just be that Trip would make it a semi-regular thing, alternating it with the steak night or the curry night, or maybe, Simon said to Ryan in a way that had sounded haughtier than he'd intended it to, maybe just one person who'd never really seen drag before, never really thought it could speak to them and to their lives, maybe just one person would see it and start to think differently about stuff. Ryan had asked him what he meant by 'differently', a smirk only half concealed, and Simon had replied, you know, just, differently.

Fieldnotes: On Leaving

Our final drive out of the town and back towards the city train station offers us a chance for reflection. We are all tired from the work we have been doing this week, emotionally as well as physically, but we feel it has been worth it. One of our party mentions the importance of debriefing in order to bring together the strands of our memories into a collective recollection of the sessions. They make the point that, without this, there is a danger of fragmenting the lessons and losing sight of the common narrative. The drive takes us through a couple of outer villages of the town before moving on to a series of roundabouts which fork off into as-yet-unfinished industrial parks.

One of our team says that if they had arrived here with no knowledge of history and no sense of previous industry it would have been easy never to find out that there had once been coal mining here. Every so often there might be an incongruous hill, an odd undulation in the land, sometimes terraced streets which seem built to serve something, or small shoebox cottages for retired workers that hint at something, but the rest is erased. Hidden. Buried.

We pass hanging baskets, each one bearing the name of a local business. We pass a sign built by volunteers out of brick that spells out a village name in black against sandstone. We are certain that the story a place tells of itself should be more important than the story that is told about it, and that the weight of the latter in national narratives silences the former. One of our team speaks up from the back of the car and asks which 'story the town might tell of itself' do we really mean? Isn't any attempt to coalesce or contain those narratives just another form of imposition? Anybody carving out small chunks of story from the wall of sound and noise and voice and memory is doing so selectively, and a small nugget of a larger thing should never be taken to be the thing itself. There is silence in the car; we seem to be in agreement.

History then, we posit, is both what is remembered and forgotten. It's the mention of the town in the Domesday Book of the eleventh century, and it's the hundreds of people who died in the 1800s in explosions at Hoyle Mill, at Lundhill. It's the public hall crush and the children suffocating and it's the explosion and the Secretary of State coming to say 'it might remind people, as it reminded me, that there is still a very high price in human life to be paid for the coal we get in this country'. It's Wombwell Main, and Houghton Main, and Newmillerdam, and Grimethorpe and Darfield Main and Cortonwood. And it's the police taking their numbers off so they could kick lumps out of picketers at Orgreave and then lying about it. But it's also tens of thousands of people, just trying to live.

We propose that, in contradiction to the popular sentiment, it's not so much that history repeats itself, it's that it crushes on, relentlessly.

Simon's right arm raised into the air, out to the side, like he's gesturing towards something. Then his left arm raised into the air, out to the side, like he's gesturing towards something. Both arms raised into the air, out to the side, like he's gesturing towards something. Like he's flung open a door. Applause, like an unroosting, a disturbance, rolling towards him, and then into him, and then beyond him.

surveillance: CCTV

Trip was finishing up in the back; there'd been some commotion when someone from the local news had turned up, too late to see the show but there to chat with Simon afterwards, but he'd eventually managed to get everyone out. It had seemed to go well, Simon enjoyed himself, and there'd definitely been more people in than usual. Different people too. Younger. He went over to switch off the computer, and saw a notification from the security cameras. Certain ones triggered an alert when anyone got within a certain range, which meant it was easier to speed through the footage if there'd been any damage, or kids messing about outside. He pulled up the clip; it was dark and so there was only the faint outline of a figure visible in the footage, approaching the door and then stopping, looking over his shoulder, back towards the road where headlights briefly lit the corner of the frame and then were gone, like a camera flash. The figure approached the door again, and then stopped again. Trip recognised the black boots, as

160

Alex stepped back into the dull glow coming from one of the windows, back into the full gaze of the camera. He was pacing, up and down the grass verge, like someone waiting for bad news. Like a bird trapped in a coop.

He stepped towards the club again, but instead of the door he went towards the window, where the camera lost clear sight of him. For a couple of minutes all Trip could see was the pavement, the grass verge, Alex's shadow thrown down onto it as light flashed from inside the club. Then Alex stepping back, into view again, seeming to look to the door once more, before walking out of frame.

They step out into the long corridor of early dawn, Brian closing the door quietly, so as not to wake their mum. They cross the road, ease open the entrance to the ginnel between the two houses and head through, the smells of last night's tea still hanging in the air like damp washing. Out the other side, Brian and Alex walk along the grass-worn-down-to-mud and turn left, into the patch of oblong trenches and tunnels. The fly-eaten cabbage, the holes the squirrels have dug around the rhubarb. They walk past the empty chair, the tumbledown shed, and head for the coop. It isn't locked. Inside, the smudges of grey and white against the early morning gloom. Alex hangs back, but Brian steps straight in, handles one, soft like a child's hair, and then turns back towards the allotment, gestures for Alex to move, and slowly opens his hands and watches it fly. And then, turning back, he opens the mesh cage, the door inside the door, and stands aside. At once they are at the entrance, all the feathers like the smoke after an explosion. Then gone; into the air, over the chimneys, across the fields. They both watch them for a moment, the way their wings rise as though they're breathing in, the long exhalation as they open to their full span, and then just the empty sky.

The TV was on in the corner of the room, but Alex wasn't really paying attention to it. 'And finally,' a voice was saying, 'the divisive figure of former prime minister Margaret Thatcher never came to Barnsley at the height of the industrial tensions of her premiership, but she was here last night, as part of a drag show put on by local resident Simon Banks.'

Alex dropped his phone into his lap, looked up at the screen. Simon was outside the club, an eager young reporter holding a microphone up to his face. 'I just think I wanted to do something a bit different. I mean she did come once, but only when she wanted our votes, before she was PM, and that was only to Penistone, so that doesn't count.'

Alex in his armchair and the presenter on TV let themselves smile at that joke; Simon saying he just wanted to entertain people, maybe make people proud. That last word stung

Alex. He knew he should have gone to see it, or rather gone inside, got something beyond the little fragments he'd seen through the window. He couldn't decide if it was worse to have gone but not be seen or not to have gone at all. His hand had been on the door but he just couldn't turn it, kept imagining Ryan on the other side of the door, waiting. He would have felt too visible. Simon's dad. Puttana-as-Thatcher's dad.

Simon was still on the TV, making the presenter laugh, gesturing back over his shoulder towards the club; he still had the wig on but his make-up had been quickly wiped away. It was too much, how Simon looked like Alex's dad, how with the wig on it was like She was still haunting him, even after the performance. Alex changed the channel; a quiz show was just coming to an end, someone was weeping, hugging the presenter, repeating over and over again that this sort of thing never happened, not to someone like them.

Alex knew he should have gone. Brian had texted him. Trip had sent him a message this morning saying he'd seen him on the cameras, and why hadn't he come in. Telling him to step up. Telling him to get over himself. There'd been nothing from Simon, which felt to Alex somehow worse. It was Ryan who'd got in touch.

Hey, it's Ryan, he'd written, knowing the number wouldn't come up on Alex's phone, *Simon would like to hear from you I think. Maybe just give him a few days like. Anyway, I haven't edited the videos of the show yet, but thought you might want to see them.*

Alex started to write a reply but stopped himself, and put the phone down. When he picked it back up there was another message from Ryan. *It's OK Alex, I'm not going to tell Simon. Let me know if you want to talk.*

A pause, and the three dots which showed Ryan was still typing. *I think you should talk to someone.*

Alex didn't reply, and instead pushed his finger against the last small square of Simon that Ryan had sent over. It became immediately larger, filling the screen.

Ryan had been filming from the back of the club, and so Simon is small, and seen over the backs of heads. Alex was pleased that the crowd looked bigger than it had through the window, hoped that meant that maybe his absence had been less conspicuous. The music, through Simon's phone into the speakers, to Ryan's camera and then out Alex's phone-speaker, was tinny, but still recognisable. It's the closing few minutes that Ryan sent over; Simon in the video spinning and ripping off a blazer to reveal a bare chest with writing on, people whooping, Ryan following his movements over to the other side of the stage and more cheering, clapping, a couple of flashes going off on camera phones.

Ryan zooms in and the picture blurs slightly but Simon is still visible, sweat running down his face, into his eyes. At one moment his hand comes up to his face as though he might wipe it away but he doesn't, and so the small rivers remain, gathering in the creases where he's smiling. And all of a sudden that song that Alex recognised coming out of the speakers: *we are women, we are strong.* The audience tapping their glasses against the table and cheering, the backs of their heads nodding along.

Simon by now was over to one side of the stage, and Ryan hadn't been able to get the camera to follow him all the way, so for a couple of minutes all Alex got from the video was the distorted noise of people singing along, Ryan's breathing, and the shadow of Simon's arm, thrown up against one of the walls of the club, a palm into a fist and then a pointing finger. Next thing Simon had moved back into the light and his whole profile, that wig, his face, was thrown onto the wall. Like a ghost, Alex thought.

Ryan re-found Simon in the middle of the stage, zooming in again, over the tops of people's heads, and Alex noticed the image shaking a bit, lifting up as Ryan rose to his tiptoes to get Simon in view. The sweat was even more obvious now, Simon's eyes wet with it as he hunched over and waved goodbye to the audience, an exaggerated look of sadness on his face. He turned a full 360 degrees, raised both his arms in the air, and bowed theatrically, before walking away to the men's toilets. The camera stayed on the empty stage for a while as people's chairs began to scrape back, chatter built up, laughter could be heard.

Alex sat for a moment, holding the phone in his hand and wishing that he'd gone and seen it, knowing that Simon would think he was embarrassed of him, ashamed. It was a pity, Alex knew. There'd been something in Simon's face, when Ryan had zoomed in, even when he was trying to look stern or upset and keep in character, his mouth kept creasing into a smile, his face brighter somehow, as though lit by the gaze of the audience. It was something Alex recognised in him from childhood, before adolescence had extinguished it; a sort of freedom, a lightness, someone purely himself.

He closed the video and, back in the text message screen, wrote *thanks* and sent it to Ryan. He switched back to the news but it was already too late; he caught the end of the reminder of the day's headline, '. . . more cuts to services', and turned the TV off entirely.

When his phone buzzed a couple of minutes later, Alex expected it to be Ryan but it was another number: eleven digits that Alex didn't have a name saved for. *Up for meeting again tonight?* the message said. Alex looked over his shoulder, out of habit, as though someone might be standing over him, reading it. There was just the window, the empty road outside.

Alex began to type out a reply, but then stopped, put the phone back, face down, on the settee. He looked over his shoulder again. Stood, both his knees cracking like a tab being pulled on a can; his breath wheezing out. He looked around the room. He'd always said that in an old house there was always something needed doing, like painting the Forth Bridge his mum used to say, something that had slipped or something that had crumbled or come loose, plaster that had settled and cracked, things readjusting themselves. Day by day, inch by inch, Alex thought to himself, the floor he was standing on, this old carpet, this very bit of ground, was not in the same place as it was yesterday.

Still, it could be worse.

sure mate, he typed, *do you want to come here?*

What to do now is clear, and wordless.
You will bear what can not be borne.

Denise Riley

Acknowledgements

Maybe a novel is a bit like a town: a single thing made possible by lots of individuals. So here are some fellow residents of Pity who need thanking.

Chris Wellbelove believed it might be possible for me to write this before I believed it myself, thanks to him and Emily Fish for taking such care with *Pity*, and to Lisa Baker, Laura Otal and Anna Hall, who helped take Barnsley to the world with their translation deals. Thanks to Francis Bickmore for giving *Pity* a home on the Canongate street, and to the whole extended team including Melissa Tombere, Lucy Zhou, Anna Frame, Jenny Fry, Alan Nevens, Vicki Rutherford, Lorraine McCann and Jamie Byng; for their patience and insights and really understanding what I was trying to do. Jon Gray created an image that said everything I'd took thousands of words to try and say, and Rachel Quin brought it wonderfully to life.

If you were to excavate back through the years, you'd eventually get back to the original source of my idea, and my interest in that word Pity, which came from studying the John Ford play *Tis Pity She's a Whore* whilst I was at Barnsley College. I was taught there by the brilliant Dr Deborah West, and I'll always be immensely grateful to her. The time to really get into the writing of this came from a research sabbatical at Manchester Metropolitan University, thanks to them, to my colleague Joe Stretch for some great early advice, and to the research teams I've been privileged to be a part of over the years, with the likes of Kate Pahl, Geoff Bright, Sarah McNicol and many other brilliant minds. Thanks too to close friends who became first close readers of the story, Okechukwu Nzelu and Seán Hewitt.

One of the final things I had to do to the proofs of this novel was to add the dates underneath the book's dedicatee, my maternal grandma Margaret Goldthorpe, who died in February 2023 at the age of 94. Maybe towns like Barnsley, and novels like this, are built on the stories and the lives of people like her. I miss her very much.

Permission Credits

Epigraph from 'Digging' in *Salutations: Collected Poems 1960–1989* by Alan Jackson. Copyright © Alan Jackson, 1990. Reproduced with permission of the Licensor through PLSclear.

Excerpts from 'A Gramophone on the Subject' in *Say Something Back* by Denise Riley. Copyright © Denise Riley, 2018. Reproduced with permission of the Licensor through PLSclear.

Epigraph from 'Looking and Finding' in *Collected Poems: Peter Scupham* by Peter Scupham. Copyright © Peter Scupham, 2002. Reproduced with permission of Carcanet Press.

Extract from '"The Lady Is Not Returning!": Educational Precarity and a Social Haunting in the UK Coalfields' by N. Geoffrey Bright. In *Ethnography and Education*, Vol. 11,